"I don't know what's ... back from Romania. ... wolf when we were there.

But after losing my job in Chicago, I'm scared I can't get the kind of job I need. Not with everybody downsizing."

A green bean snapped in the silence. "It's okay," Carrie said. "You're allowed to ask questions. Just keep trusting the Lord."

The door opened, and Steve burst in with their boy, Viktor. He dumped a couple of bags on the table. "How's my favorite wife?" Steve hugged Carrie as if he hadn't seen her in days, not hours. *Oh God, will I ever find someone like that?*

Joe. Michelle pushed the thought away. She had no business thinking like that about a man she met only last night—and certainly not with her other obligations. But when she remembered his infectious grin, ready laugh, and gentle touch, the idea thrilled her. *Stop it*, she scolded herself. Her heart didn't want to listen.

Award-winning author and speaker **DARLENE FRANKLIN** recently returned to cowboy country—Oklahoma. The move was prompted by her desire to be close to her son's family; her daughter Jolene has preceded her into glory.

Darlene loves music, needlework, reading, and reality TV. Talia, a lynx point Siamese cat, proudly claims Darlene as her person.

Darlene has published several titles with Barbour Publishing. Visit Darlene's blog at www.darlenefranklin-writes.blogspot.com for information on book giveaways and upcoming titles.

Books by Darlene Franklin

HEARTSONG PRESENTS
HP650—Romanian Rhapsody
HP855—Beacon of Love
HP911—The Prodigal Patriot
HP931—Bridge to Love
HP947—Love's Raid

Plainsong

Darlene Franklin

Heartsong Presents

A special thanks to Kathy Brasby for helping me with the layout of Coors Field and to Regina Jennings, Erin Young, and Sharon Srock for helping me bring this "child" to birth.

A note from the Author:
I love to hear from my readers! You may correspond with me by writing:

Darlene Franklin
Author Relations
PO Box 721
Uhrichsville, OH 44683

ISBN 978-1-61626-363-8

PLAINSONG

Scripture quotations are taken from the HOLY BIBLE, NEW INTERNATIONAL VERSION®. NIV®. Copyright © 1973, 1978, 1984, 2010 by Biblica, Inc.™ Used by permission. All rights reserved worldwide.

Scripture taken from the New King James Version®. Copyright © 1982 by Thomas Nelson, Inc. Used by permission. All rights reserved.

Our mission is to publish and distribute inspirational products offering exceptional value and biblical encouragement to the masses.

PRINTED IN THE U.S.A.

one

"Do you want to know the way to heaven?" A young man dressed in a suit coat and tie, unexpected on the hot July night, asked people as they surged past him to Coors Field for a night of Colorado Rockies baseball. Before walking on, Joe Knight glanced at the tract with a bright red cross on it.

"You're not interested in heaven then?" The man's voice trailed after him.

Joe stopped to explain that he already knew the way to heaven and to wish the evangelist Godspeed, but the man had already turned his attention elsewhere. Joe shook his head as he watched the man approach an attractive young woman. She flicked sweeping blond hair over her shoulder as she accepted the tract and stopped for a minute to talk. Joe took in her long, shapely legs and well-tailored slacks.

Coins jangled nearby, and one of the street bums who cluttered every corner stopped Joe. His sign read HOMELESS VET. PLEASE HELP. How much money had he stashed away during the course of the day? Joe had heard news reports about the scams some of the street people pulled. The woman he had seen before approached, dug in her purse, and tossed in a handful of change.

Joe hesitated then followed her. "Ma'am, I wouldn't do that again if I were you."

She turned deep green eyes in his direction. "Excuse me?"

For a moment he forgot what he was saying, and then he found his voice. "That man. He'll probably just use the money for alcohol or drugs."

"Or maybe he'll buy a meal. He could use one. There's no reason people should go hungry in a rich country like America." Her eyes clouded.

She turned away, and Joe noticed a couple behind her who looked vaguely familiar.

"Joe Knight, what brings you all the way to Denver tonight?" the husband asked.

His brain made the connection. "Steve and Carrie— Romero, isn't it? I'm in town on business but had tickets to the game tonight. What a surprise to run into you here. But I don't believe I've had the privilege of meeting your friend."

Carrie turned to the stunning blond. "Michelle, this is Joe Knight. Joe is on the mission committee of one of the churches that supports the work in Romania. And Joe, this is my friend, Michelle Morris."

Green eyes fastened on his face. "That's wonderful." She extended a manicured hand. "I was in Romania at the same time Carrie was. That's where we met."

Was Michelle a missionary as well? I'd like to learn more about her. He felt for the baseball tickets stashed in his pocket, given to him when one of his clients couldn't go to the game. *Why not?* "Ma'am?"

She glanced at him again, her smile questioning. "Yes?"

"Do you like baseball?"

"I love it. I'm afraid I'm the one who dragged Carrie and Steve here tonight." She glanced at the brunette.

"Although we're headed for the rock pile," Carrie said. "Not the best seats."

"Well." Joe paused. *What would she think of a total stranger inviting her out? I'll never know unless I ask.* "I have an extra ticket along the right field line to tonight's game. It's the Mets." He waved the tickets as if the Yankees were in town. "Would you like to join me?"

Michelle took stock of the handsome man in front of her. He was tall—taller than her own five-ten in stockinged feet—good-looking in a cowboy kind of way, well-spoken.

Her friend Carrie nudged her elbow. "Go ahead. You'll have a better view of the game. We can catch up with you later."

When Michelle still hesitated, Carrie pulled her aside and whispered, "He's single and he's Christian, and he loves baseball. Go for it." They smiled at each other. Ever since Carrie's marriage to the widowed Steve Romero, she'd been bent on making a match for her friend.

Michelle faced the stranger. *At least he can look me in the eye.* She hated being taller than the man she was dating. "I accept." She waved good-bye to Carrie and turned to face the mysterious Mr. Knight.

"Have fun," Carrie called over her shoulder as they headed for the turnstiles.

"We'll meet you by the front gate after the game," Steve added.

"Are you visiting Steve and Carrie?" Joe asked.

"I'm thinking about moving here, but I'm just visiting at the moment, from Chicago. You? You don't live in Denver?"

"I lived here for a while. Now I make my home in the great metropolis of Ulysses, out on the eastern plains." He guided her through the sea of Rockies purple, silver, and black that swam toward the gates.

Hundreds of people strolled down the sidewalks, fathers and sons, mothers with babies dressed in miniature uniforms, old men in faded caps. Michelle watched the crowd, fascinated. "It's like a parade. Or a town fair—or something."

"Yeah, it's a lot of fun. One of the few things I miss about Denver."

A lone clarinet sang above the noise of the crowd, serenading them with "Take Me Out to the Ball Game." Joe tossed a couple of bills into the collection hat. "How about 'God Bless America' for the lady?"

"Anything you say." The old performer slid into the patriotic hit, swaying in time to the music.

Michelle clapped, delighted. "That was wonderful. Thanks." She added some change to the hat.

"Do you mind if we buy some snacks out here? More choices than inside. Cheaper, too." Joe grinned.

"Lead the way."

Joe led her to a table piled high with every conceivable snack they might want at the game. He grabbed a bottle of cold water and a box of Cracker Jacks.

Michelle did her own exploring. Peanuts? No. "Pistachios. And Gummi Bears. And Circus Peanuts. How can I choose?"

"Take them all." Joe grabbed everything Michelle had mentioned.

The vendor, a black man with a grin inviting them to join the Rockies' party, made change for Joe. A few seconds later, they rejoined the thousands streaming toward the main gate.

"Get your programs here."

"Caps, only five dollars each. Ten dollars inside."

It's like the whole city is having a party. What a wonderful place to visit. Another reason I'm glad I'm moving to Denver. Michelle stopped, savoring the atmosphere, but Joe took her by the hand and pulled her toward the turnstiles.

Pounding music poured from the loudspeakers as they made their way to their seats along the right outfield line. A jumbo screen over center field featured spectacular plays by Rockies players. They crawled over a dozen people to the center of the row.

"Good. We made it in time," Joe said, taking a swig from

his water bottle. "I hate it when I miss the first inning. Sometimes by the time I get settled, the opposing team has already scored three runs." Almost as an afterthought, he offered, "Can I get you something to drink?"

Michelle chuckled inwardly. At least he asked. "I have my bottle of water here. Maybe later. They're about to start."

True to Joe's experience, the Mets' lead-off hitter blasted a home run into right field. Beside her, Joe sighed. "Looks like we're in for one of those games. If you like home runs, it's great."

"Oh yes, much more exciting than a pitchers' duel anytime—don't you think?" She poked him with her elbow.

Eyes dancing in merry disagreement, he said, "Maybe. Especially if I can catch one of the balls."

Surveying the packed stadium, Michelle laughed. "Do you really think you have a chance? Are they going to send one to you special delivery?"

"I can always hope." He reached into his gym bag and pulled out a catcher's mitt.

A beer vendor hawked his wares, but Joe ignored him. Instead he purchased a couple of iced lemonades. They didn't talk much until the top of the inning was over. The Mets had scored two runs.

"Have you been in Denver long?" Joe asked.

Michelle shook her head. "Only a few days. I love it so far. I'm staying with the Romeros while I look for a job." *If I get a job. Lord, help!*

"I hope I didn't disrupt their plans for the evening."

"Oh, they won't mind." Michelle smiled, thinking of the dates she had talked over with Carrie while they were missionaries together in Romania. What would she say about the man next to her tonight? So far, so good. "What about you? You said you used to live in Denver. Why did you leave?"

"A family emergency." Joe's lips flattened momentarily. "An opportunity came up to open a business in Ulysses. I took the chance, and it's starting to pay off. Ah, the Rockies are up to bat now. This is a new guy. Haven't seen him before."

Minutes later, with two batters on base, the cleanup hitter came to the plate.

"Here's my chance." Joe slipped his glove onto his left hand.

Michelle stared curiously.

"He's almost as good as the old Blake Street Bombers. Hits a lot of home runs. He's the best there is at hitting with men on base. This may be my chance to snag one."

Around her Michelle felt anticipation growing. The jumbo screen flashed the hitter's name, with the crowd screaming in time to the syllables. He stepped into the batter's box, and a hush fell on the stadium.

The first pitch was a ball, the second a called strike. On the third, Michelle heard the crack of the bat. The ball hurtled in their direction, and the batter raced down the first-base line.

An older woman next to them squealed and ducked. "I'll protect you, ma'am." Joe waved his arm in front of him. Around them other men were doing the same thing. Michelle couldn't pick out his arm from the sea awaiting the ball. Joe leaped in the air.

"Got it!" Triumphantly he twisted his glove around to show Michelle the prized ball. All three Rockies players trotted home, putting the team ahead 3–2. Joe's image appeared on the jumbo screen, and he grinned like he'd won the World Series. Waving his arms in the air like a conquering hero, he pulled a laughing Michelle to her feet beside him. Around him men were high-fiving him.

"Good catch."

"Maybe I can get it autographed." Joe wiggled back into

the seat. "You must be my good-luck charm. I've never managed to catch one before." He bounced the ball in his hand and looked at Michelle, warmth flooding his eyes. "I want you to have it." Taking Michelle's hands between his own, he gently rolled the ball into her palm.

"But. I can't take it. You just said—"

"No arguing. Maybe I'll catch another one. I want you to enjoy it."

"Thanks." Michelle closed her fingers around it, savoring the weight of the tiny packed ball, imagining it on her shelf next to the pennant autographed by Chicago Cubs all-stars, a memento of one of her favorite childhood memories. "That was quite a performance."

Joe grinned a bit sheepishly and opened his game program. "Three-run homer. That should be easy to mark."

Michelle peered over his shoulder at the bewildering chart of lines, x's, and numbers he held, much more complicated than a bowling score sheet. "You know, I've been to lots of games, but I've never tried keeping track of the plays like that."

"It's pretty easy. Let me show you."

The innings slipped by, Joe arguing calls by the umpire, mentioning tidbits of Rockies lore, showing Michelle how to keep score. By the seventh-inning stretch, her voice was hoarse from cheering awesome catches and groaning over foul balls. The game organ struck familiar opening chords. Joe dragged her to her feet.

"You have to sing."

Words flashed on the jumbo screen. All the fun of the evening raced through Michelle's veins and burst out in a wide smile. Buoyant high spirits cracked Joe's face into a matching grin.

Catching her hands, he swung her arms in time to the

music. "Take me out to the ball game," they sang at the top of their lungs. Michelle couldn't hold a tune, but she didn't care if anyone heard her or not. "For it's one, two, three strikes. . ." They punched fingers emphatically in the air. The jumbo screen showed fans all over the stadium dancing to the music. They held out the last note as long as they could and collapsed in their seats, laughing.

The Rockies hadn't scored since the home run in the first inning, while the Mets piled up a 7-3 lead.

"It doesn't look good," Michelle said as the first Rockies hitter struck out in the bottom of the seventh inning.

"I've seen 'em come from six—even nine—runs down late in the game. Four runs, that's nothing," Joe said comfortably. "Hey, you want to walk around a bit? It's a beautiful place."

Michelle nodded, and they made their way out of the stands. Souvenirs like plastic bats, autographed balls, caps, and pennants from teams across the league filled booths as far as she could see.

"Who's your favorite team? The Cubs or the White Sox?"

"The Cubs. My Dad took me to opening day every year when I was growing up. He said that was the only game worth watching, since the Cubs' two seasons are spring training and next year."

Joe laughed.

"Did you grow up a Rockies fan? Or did you grow up somewhere else?"

"Well, I'm not from Denver, but I remember the excitement when we got the baseball team. I am a native Coloradoan, though. One of the few, I think. Ah, I smell hot dogs up ahead."

The delicious aroma convinced Michelle to try one with Joe, although she didn't think they tasted quite as good as ones she'd had in Chicago. They never did. They meandered down the concourse, stopping at each booth. Michelle wondered at the warm winter jackets that looked so out of place on the hot summer night. Ahead of them a commotion broke out.

"Hey. Stop. Thief!" A vendor with heavy jowls burst from behind his stall. "Security!"

A blue-garbed officer rushed to his aid. "What's up?"

"Catch him! A white guy, a kid, about five-ten, five-eleven. Braves hat."

Michelle stared in the direction the man pointed but saw no sign of the thief in the crowds. The guard ran after him anyway.

The vendor shook his head. "Vandals. Here at the ballpark. I mean, once in a while a kid walks off with a ball, but this was...this was..." He couldn't finish the sentence.

"I'm sorry." Michelle was tempted to buy something, as if she could make up for the loss. She looked around for Joe, but he had left her side.

He'd sprinted after the security guard.

two

"So he took off running after the thief?" Carrie shook her head in disbelief as Michelle related the story.

"Sure did." Michelle stared straight ahead, eyes unfocused, slowly sipping the cup of Good Night Tea Carrie had fixed for her. "They caught him, too."

"Really?" Carrie leaned forward, elbows sticking out of her housecoat and resting on the table.

"Yeah. A few minutes later they brought this scruffy-looking teenager back in handcuffs and escorted him to the gate. Joe looked pleased as punch with himself." She stirred a third teaspoon of sugar into the tea and sipped it. Her nose wrinkled at the overly sweet taste, and she pushed the cup away.

"I wonder if he's always that impulsive."

"I'd say so." Michelle extracted the ball from her purse. "Did you see when he caught that home-run ball in the first inning?"

"Oh yeah! What a catch."

"He gave me the ball."

"Impulsive. Generous." Carrie ticked off the qualities as if she were making a shopping list. "That boyish quality that can make men so sweet."

"Yes." The two women sighed in tandem.

"So when are you seeing him again?" Carrie grinned.

"The day after tomorrow. He's taking me to the Cherry Creek Arts Festival. I told him I had to work on my résumé after church tomorrow."

❧

Michelle ran her finger down the list of Denver's hundred

largest employers again. Where should she start?

"Why don't you try a placement agency?" Carrie snapped green beans.

"Maybe later," Michelle said. "But human resources is supposed to be my area of expertise. If I can't find a job for myself, how can I expect a company to trust me with their personnel decisions?" Studying the list again, she crossed out a few more lines. No beer companies, medicine-related, or sports. Legal? Maybe. Computers? Not enough people contact. Communications. "I'd like that." She marked her top five choices with bold red stars. "I'll start with these."

"Now for my résumé." She looked at the large amount of white space surrounding the few lines of type and sighed. "It would help if I had more experience. Part-time jobs in college, two years in Romania, that last job in Chicago. Nothing related to my supposed career, except for that last one that I lost when they downsized."

"You can't get down on yourself since that job didn't work out. People are people, whether in Romania or Denver." Carrie had emptied one sack of green beans and reached for another. "And you have cross-cultural experience. You have a lot to offer."

"But is it what they're looking for?" Michelle studied the résumé without inspiration. "I reviewed tons of these in school, learning what to watch for. I want to look professional. I know I can do better than this." She tapped her pen against her teeth. "I know—I'll mention working at my father's store."

"That's a good idea. I'm sure you learned a lot about customer relations and dealing with the public." Carrie examined a green bean and threw it away.

"The customers were the best part." Michelle smiled at the memory. "Like old Mrs. Westlake. She'd stop by every day for a pint of milk. Dad said she liked my company. She didn't really need anything." She added a few lines to the résumé and read it again. "I need to make the sentences active. Show them what I actually did." She rewrote several lines. "There. I'm done."

"Let me see." Carrie read the revisions. "That ought to wow 'em. They'll be knocking down the door."

"That's the idea." Michelle decided she had done as much as she could and printed out several copies. "I don't know what's happened to me since I got back from Romania. I had the courage of a she-wolf when we were there. But after losing my job in Chicago, I'm scared I can't get the kind of job I need. Not with everybody downsizing."

A green bean snapped in the silence. "It's okay," Carrie said. "You're allowed to ask questions. Just keep trusting the Lord."

The door opened, and Steve burst in with their boy, Viktor. He dumped a couple of bags on the table. "How's my favorite wife?" Steve hugged Carrie as if he hadn't seen her in days, not hours. *Oh God, will I ever find someone like that?*

Joe. Michelle pushed the thought away. She had no business thinking like that about a man she met only last night—and certainly not with her other obligations. But when she remembered his infectious grin, ready laugh, and gentle touch, the idea thrilled her. *Stop it*, she scolded herself. Her heart didn't want to listen.

ᨠ

Joe woke up early, even though he had tossed and turned all night. Hotel rooms always did that to him. Or was it the prospect of seeing Michelle again? Yesterday had dragged by, but he had filled in some of the time by calling home to make sure his mother didn't need anything.

Michelle. Her name rolled off his tongue and lingered in his mind, a beautiful name for a beautiful woman. Their date at the game had confirmed his first impressions of her.

Why had he invited Michelle to go to the arts festival with him? The last thing he needed while he conducted business was a date with a city girl—even one as pretty as Michelle.

Even with a long shower and careful grooming, he slipped behind the wheel of his truck before eight—forty-five minutes before he would pick up Michelle. He ran his finger over the tooled-leather wheel cover while he decided what to do. He drove around the city, catching up on changes, until his watch read 8:30. Time to head south to the place Michelle was staying.

He recognized the house from Michelle's description: a modest ranch house with a nearly new play set visible in the backyard. A small boy sat on the swing, kicking the ground with his feet. Joe waved to him.

Grabbing his cowboy hat with one hand and opening the door with the other, he jumped out into the oppressive sunshine of another midsummer day. He tucked a stray patch of shirt back into his pants and headed to the front door.

&

"Where did he get that hat? He'll think I'm too dressed up." Michelle frowned nervously at her aqua knit shell and navy blue linen slacks.

"He does look like he stepped off the set of *Gunsmoke*." Carrie shrugged. Her husband, Steve, wasn't the cowboy-hat-and-boots type. As if sensing Michelle's unease, she added, "You look great. He'll think you're beautiful."

"I'll change into one of my patriotic tees. It *is* almost the Fourth of July after all. Tell him I'll be right back."

When she came back a few minutes later, she hesitated when she saw him chatting with Carrie. He must have sensed her presence, for he turned sapphire blue eyes in her direction. An electric jolt coursed through her, tingling down to her toes. "Good morning, Joe." Breathless, she sounded like a high-school girl.

Joe's eyes slid up and down her body, smiling at what he saw, until he frowned at her feet. "You might want walking shoes. We'll be on our feet all day."

"I'm used to it." She didn't have to defend wearing heels. She couldn't explain the sense of style, of feeling attractive and feminine, that the navy pumps gave her. Tossing a chain purse over her shoulder, she said, "I'm ready. Bye, Carrie. See you tonight."

A dusty blue truck waited in the driveway, and her heart quailed a bit. Trucks seemed more common than cars in Denver. The things she was learning about the West.

"Let me help you." Joe swung the door open and offered his arm for support. Accepting it, she lifted her left heel onto the floor of the cab and slid onto the seat. He circled the vehicle and swung onto the driver's seat with one easy movement.

When he turned the key in the ignition, a wailing love song blasted for a moment before he turned the radio off.

Country music?

Returning to the main street by a route Michelle had never taken before, Joe headed down Federal Boulevard. "You seem to know Denver pretty well."

"I should. Lived here for three years."

"You've been to this festival before, then? Tell me about it."

"Somebody came up with the idea a long time ago. You may know that Cherry Creek is kind of a yuppie mall. Someone wanted to add to the highbrow tone, and they decided to sponsor an arts festival around the Fourth of July to showcase local talent, both artists and musicians. It's grown to the point where people come from across the country to attend."

"You must like art to travel to Denver for the festival."

Joe made a noncommittal grunt. They turned into a residential neighborhood then turned by a church. Soon they reached barriers festooned with yellow flags. "Here we are. The edge of Cherry Creek North."

A young woman dressed in crisp blue slacks and a white blouse with a red and blue bowtie approached. "Do you want me to park your car, sir?"

"Please." Joe handed her a twenty-dollar bill.

Michelle stared down the ordinary city street transformed into an art market. Red and white tents crowded both sides, stretching ahead for as many blocks as she could see. Artisans called greetings to each other while they opened their tents and arranged their wares for maximum effect. The sight reminded her a bit of the early-morning bustle of the street markets in Bucharest. Warm memories engulfed her.

"—breakfast?"

Michelle brought her attention back to Joe. "I'm sorry. What did you say?"

"Things won't get started for a half hour yet. Would you like some breakfast?"

"Oh, sure." She was a little surprised when he guided her to a bagel and coffee shop. Somehow pancakes with bacon and eggs seemed more Joe's style.

Michelle ordered a tall latte, iced, with skim milk, and a whole-grain bagel, light on the cream cheese. They found an empty spot at a corner table, and Joe crunched into the toasted onion bagel with a thick layer of cream cheese.

Michelle opened her bagel and took a small bite. At home she often used ricotta as a spread, but at restaurants she allowed the indulgence.

"There's nothing like an onion bagel with cream cheese." A dollop of the filling fell onto the plate, and Joe scooped it into his mouth. "Yummy."

It really was. Michelle took a bigger bite the next time. A piece fell off.

"Let me." Joe brushed the renegade crumb away from Michelle's cheek. His fingers were surprisingly soft and supple, a gentle caress of a touch. Her skin heated to his touch, and she hastened to change the topic.

"This bunch doesn't look anything like the crowd at Coors Field." Not with Gucci shirts and Italian shoes. "I began to think everyone in Denver dressed casually—or in gear from their favorite sports star."

Joe leaned back and laughed, a warm, comfortable chuckle. "Not true." He leaned close. "You have to come to Ulysses for that." He winked at her, and she giggled.

They finished their bagels and ventured back onto the street. Already a couple of hundred people milled around the stalls. The artist in the tent across from the café caught sight of Joe and waved in greeting before rearranging her glassware on the front table a fraction of an inch.

"Ready?" At Michelle's nod, he headed across the street.

"Good morning, Annie. What have you got today?" Joe greeted the middle-aged artist, who sported soft brown hair pulled back in a braid.

"You might be interested in this." She pulled out a thin bud vase made of pale gold-blown glass.

Joe bent down and looked at his luminous reflection in the glass before showing it to Michelle. "It's different from your usual work."

"Yes, I'm using different materials. . . ." Annie relaxed as she described how she created the new effect.

Michelle admired the pieces in the booth. Exquisite, delicate work, they would complement a lot of the renovated turn-of-the-century homes dotted around Denver. Joe's voice interrupted her perusal.

"Annie, I'd like you to meet my friend, Michelle Morris. Michelle, Annie is an old business associate of mine." Introductions completed, he made arrangements to come back later and pick up a couple of pieces.

"Are you a collector?" Michelle was curious.

"You mean Annie?" Joe seemed bemused. "No, not a collector. It's my business."

"You mean. . ." The light dawned for Michelle. "Your business in Ulysses. You own an art gallery? Or a museum?"

"Gallery. Buy direct from the artists, resell at my store. Ah, here's Jonah's shop. He makes interesting things out of wood."

The morning continued in much the same vein. Joe stopped at every tent. Michelle would have skipped a few, like the Georgia O'Keeffe–type flowers and the sculptures of twisted metal. But Joe examined every piece with an appraiser's eye.

Pictures of tall mountains and meadows teeming with wildflowers filled one tent. Michelle studied them, absorbed in the play of light in the paintings. "I wish I could buy this one." The price tag of $1,000 was far more than she could afford.

"Really?" Joe studied the painting with her. "It's kind of derivative."

"Maybe that's what I like about it. It reminds me of paintings by Charles Russell." When he lifted an eyebrow at her, she said, "What? I've heard of Russell, even in Chicago."

Joe cocked his head and looked over the painting, his finger tracing the brush strokes in the air. "You may be right. And it's a popular site in Colorado, the Maroon Bells. I'll think about it."

A few tents later, Joe surprised Michelle by asking her about an abstract painting vibrant with angry reds and yellows. "What do you think?"

"It would give me headaches hanging on my wall." The words blurted out of Michelle's mouth before she thought of the artist standing within hearing distance. His mouth thinned to a tense line.

Joe turned to study the painting from a different angle. "It's powerful, though. It's hard to look away." Nothing else in the tent interested him, and they left, Joe promising to think about the painting.

Michelle wouldn't admit that her heeled feet hurt, but she wanted a break from the serious pursuit of art. She should be glad her escort took his time; so many men avoided art museums altogether or rushed through at hiking speed without bothering to look at anything. But shopping with Joe was a bit like watching meat marinate. Nothing happened for a long time.

A few feet away she heard the sweet notes of a soprano saxophone. She tapped Joe's elbow. "I'll be over there." She found a spot at the back of the staged area. A thin black man, noticing her rub her heels, offered her a seat. Gratefully she sank down and let the music carry her away. Eyes closed, she could imagine she was sitting on the shores of Lake Michigan on a perfect day, sun dancing on the waves and wind rippling lightly through the air and curling her hair around her face. The music felt as cool as that breeze.

"Michelle?" Joe's voice intruded, jolting her back to the hot sticky July day. "It looks like you're ready for a break. How about fresh-squeezed lemonade and some real music?" His voice had music in it, too—music that drew her to her feet like she was hypnotized.

Michelle stayed rooted to the spot for a moment, and he gently tugged her arm. The saxophonist launched into the rendition of one of her favorites, and Michelle said, "Can we come back later?"

A surprised look darted across Joe's face. "Sure. Why don't you grab one of those schedules and decide. But they're starting karaoke down at the country-western stage. That's always fun to watch."

Karaoke. Oh no.

Grabbing her hand like a toddler on a field trip, he bounced through the crowded streets to the spot where a guitar twanged and voices wailed.

A tall, tanned man dressed in the cowboy uniform of boots, blue jeans, and a ten-gallon hat, with silver points decorating the collar of his denim shirt, announced, "Our next contestant will sing the Hank Williams' classic, 'Your Cheatin' Heart.'"

Michelle resigned herself to enduring the set. Country music had never appealed to her. Southern twang and clanging chords drowned out everything else as far as she was concerned. Joe obviously felt differently.

Beside her, Joe swayed in time to the music. "You can't go wrong with Hank Williams." His voice joined the performer's along with many others in the crowd.

Unable to resist the infectious enthusiasm of the crowd, Michelle found herself clapping her hands and tapping her feet. *I can understand the words.* A change from most popular music she heard on the radio. The next performer sang a couple of songs that brought tears to her eyes.

"This doesn't sound like any country I've heard before." She dabbed at her eyes.

"Still the great living, loving, and leaving songs they've always been. Real-life stuff."

A cowgirl took the mike and announced, "We have time for a couple more numbers. Any volunteers?"

Joe pirouetted in his seat, bouncing with fun. "You want to give it a try?"

"I don't know any country songs." Her insides trembled at the thought of performing in front of all those people.

"Bet you know your American history, though." Joe had her on her feet, sauntering down the center aisle in time to the clapping crowd. "It *is* almost the Fourth of July after all." He winked at her.

He told the sound technicians, "We're going to try 'The Battle of New Orleans.'" A couple of chords blasted over the loudspeakers, and Michelle found herself on stage with a microphone stuck in her hand, words rolling down a screen to her right. The *rat-a-tat* of a drum set her foot tapping.

"In 1814 we took a little trip. . . ." Joe started singing a melody that sounded vaguely familiar, his voice a pleasant baritone. The microphone dangled from Michelle's hand. When he got to the chorus, he motioned for Michelle to join in. Nothing for it but to go ahead.

"We fired our guns, and the British kept a-comin'. . . ." Joe pumped his arms, urging the audience to sing along. He skipped around her, grinning as widely as the brim of his hat. She returned the favor as he sang the second verse, clapping her hands over her head in time to the music. Minutes later the song ended, and she came back down to earth, face red-hot, breathless. The audience clapped wildly as they exited the stage.

&

She's a lot of fun when she lets her hair down. Joe loved hamming it up—he had considered pursuing a career as a musician but decided he just wasn't good enough. Every now and then he allowed himself to step back into the limelight, like today. He appreciated the break from the serious business negotiations that had dominated the morning. Michelle was a good sport, playing right along with him. They laughed together as they joined the crowds walking among the booths.

"Joe?"

The voice pierced, pinning him to the ground where he stood.

"It *is* you. I thought I heard your voice, Sir Cameron."

Joe winced. His past had caught up with him.

three

Joe deliberately relaxed his facial muscles before he turned around to greet his old girlfriend. "Sonia. I didn't see your name on the list."

She came up and kissed him on the cheek. "I don't have a booth, if that's what you mean." She tightened the knot of the brightly colored scarf draped around her hips. "But I wouldn't miss the festival. An artist has to keep an eye on the competition, you know." She flashed bright teeth in Michelle's direction. "And who is your charming friend?"

"I'm Michelle Morris." She held out her hand in greeting. "I'm new in Denver, and Joe was kind enough to offer to show me around today." She paused. "But who is Sir Cameron?"

Joe shuffled his feet, but Sonia laughed. "Why, Joe, of course. He hasn't told you about the castle yet?" When Michelle shook her head, Sonia said, "Don't worry. He will." She flashed white teeth in his direction. "And I'm Sonia Oliveira. Joe and I, uh, used to date."

Joe didn't know how to respond. Explain that Joseph was his middle name? Escape from Sonia before the situation became even more complicated?

But Michelle seemed at ease in the awkward situation. He watched the two women, noting the contrasts between his former girlfriend and his current interest. Both were tall, independent, articulate, fun—but there the similarities ended. Michelle was a gentle summer rain where Sonia was a thunderstorm, tasteful style versus artistic flamboyance. Sonia never needed encouragement to let her hair down.

"Can you come by my studio while you're in town? You promised the next time you came to Denver. . ."

Joe scrambled to remember his last conversation with Sonia. He did remember some kind of vague promise to that effect. "I'm pretty busy."

"I'll be in this evening, say, after seven? I've got some pieces I think you will want to handle." Sonia beamed a beguiling smile his way.

Joe heard himself agreeing to the time. With a sinking heart, he realized how much he'd hoped that he and Michelle could go somewhere to relax after the festival shut down—a quiet restaurant, maybe, where they could make small talk and learn more about each other. He sneaked a glance at Michelle, her face unreadable. No clue if she had any regrets about Sonia's suggestion.

Sonia made polite excuses and took off. Not a moment too soon, as far as Joe was concerned.

The scent of hot dogs on the grill tickled Joe's nose, and he realized he was hungry. He didn't want frankfurters again, though, not after the ball game last night. Michelle had wandered into a leather-goods booth, examining the stitches on some purses.

"Sorry about the interruption." Why did he feel he had to apologize? Sonia was an old flame, that was why.

"It's fine. I understand." The edge to her voice suggested perhaps she had had enough of taking care of business. Joe resolved to let go of the rest of the day's planned itinerary and to enjoy himself with this beautiful woman. First order of business: lunch.

≈

Michelle slipped her feet back into her heels and pushed away from the table. Her feet had rested while her taste buds savored the delicate blend of Chinese cuisine they had ordered.

"Ready?" Joe tossed an after-dinner mint in her direction. "I have a great idea. . . ."

"More country karaoke?" Michelle smiled. "Or maybe jazz this time?"

"Neither. Come on, you'll see."

As soon as they exited the air-conditioned restaurant, oven-hot air blasted her face, melting whatever makeup remained from the morning. Temperatures must have been close to a hundred degrees. She was glad she had put on sunscreen that morning, or else she'd be lobster-red by late afternoon. If she had some with her, she might even add a fresh coat.

Twice as many people crowded the streets as in the morning, but Joe wove his way through the foot traffic as if heading for a specific destination. They approached a booth with a long line of waiting children. "Here is one of my favorite artists. Gil is famous for his body art, but he volunteers his services at the festival."

Body art was an understatement. Michelle could hardly keep from staring at the vines, flowers, and animals that crawled up the artist's massive arms to a pirate's ring dangling from his left ear. An incongruous assortment of water, colors, and sponges lay on a table before him, and the sign over the booth announced FACE PAINTING. Face painting? Surely children would run the other way when they saw this rough giant. But a couple of young girls perched on high stools, giggling as he put finishing touches on matching unicorns.

Joe crouched, studying the featured designs hanging from the front of the booth. "What do you think, Michelle? Maybe a cowboy hat for me and—"

"You can't be serious. This is for children."

"No it's not." He pointed to a mother walking away with her daughter, both of them with matching roses on their cheeks. Joe grinned and took a place in line.

When Michelle glanced around, she saw a handful of adults waiting their turn and relaxed. The young boy ahead of them chose a dinosaur.

"My son loves dinosaurs, too." The deep voice surprised Michelle with its soft gentleness. Gil held a purple paint stick crayon with the delicate touch of an artist, deftly creating a T-rex as the child squirmed under tickling fingers.

"What do you think?" Gil showed the boy his reflection in a mirror.

"I love it." The boy flung his arms around Gil's neck, reminding Michelle of her pastor-mentor in Romania, a man who loved children. She swallowed the lump in her throat.

"Joe, my friend." The two men embraced. "What can I do for you today?" Michelle could almost hear Gil mentally rubbing his hands together. He leaned back in his chair, studying both of them in turn. "No, don't tell me. I know what you need. Who's first?"

Michelle shook her head, and with a shrug Joe perched atop a high stool, one toe dragging the ground. What kind of face did Gil have in mind for Joe?

Joe wiggled his eyebrows as Gil applied a base of white paint. White everywhere—forehead, cheeks, chin, only skipping the nose, until Joe resembled a street mime. An orange triangle on his chin pointed to his lips, bright yellow circles spotted his cheeks, and blue ringed his eyes. Joe started to grin but stopped when the paint smudged around his mouth. Add a green wig and big red nose, and he'd be set to join the circus. His eyes followed Gil's movements, causing the rings to seem to twirl. Michelle covered her mouth and turned her head to keep from laughing out loud.

Gil finished the nose in bright red. Michelle couldn't meet Joe's eyes. In spite of her best efforts, a giggle bubbled up through her throat, exiting in a tiny snicker.

"What have you done?" Joe grabbed the mirror and studied his face. He didn't bother holding back, letting out a loud belly laugh. "You know me too well." When he wiped the tears of laughter from his eyes, blue circles contracted in the effort, and he smeared paint on his knuckles.

Michelle reached into her purse for a tissue and wiped the offending paint away, giggles escaping in spite of her best efforts.

"Okay, your turn next." Joe guided her onto the seat, her heel catching on a rung of the stool.

"Oh no." Michelle tried to get off.

Gil and Joe stared at her, waiting, as children behind them stirred.

"You can't get out of it now. Turnabout's fair play."

I guess I have to go through with it. "Just no clown for me, please?" she said in a small voice. She hadn't done anything like this since she was a child herself.

"Never a clown for the lady." Gil selected an assortment of paint sticks in soft pastels. "You will like what I have in mind—I promise."

"Let's see if he knows you as well as he knows me," Joe said. "He has a way of seeing into people."

Unlikely—we just met. Instead of applying an overall base, Gil dabbed a small sponge in brown and black paint and made a long streak down her right cheek. The cool water in the sponge made Michelle's pores close up, and she forced herself to stay still under Gil's fingers. Greens, blues, pinks, and lavenders followed in quick succession. She tried to picture the patterns he was making, but she couldn't guess. When Gil brushed her hair behind her ear, she twisted in her seat.

"Don't worry. I'm almost done." A few strokes later, he put down the sponge and held up the mirror.

Whatever Michelle had expected, her imagination hadn't come close to the garden blooming on her face. Trees and flowers à la Monet adorned her cheek, leaves and branches circling her ear. The colors glowed on her skin like a makeup artist's palette, highlighting her coloring and complementing her outfit. She almost wished she wouldn't have to wash it away that evening.

Joe appeared in front of her, producing a pink rose with a magician's sleight of hand. "To the prettiest flower in the garden." He bowed.

Gil stood back, a wide grin indicating his pleasure with the result.

"Thanks. I don't know what I expected, but nothing like this. You've made me feel beautiful."

Joe's grin said "I told you so" as loudly as if he spoke out loud.

"You *are* beautiful, on the inside as well." Gil waved away payment. "Just tell people who did the work. You're walking advertising."

Michelle slid off the stool, cupping her cheek with her hand, almost expecting a flower to drop into her palm, and followed Joe into the crowd.

❧

Joe watched Michelle's transformation. The elaborate design might have looked out of place on someone else, but on her it only emphasized what was already there. Even better, she seemed to realize it, her back a fraction straighter, her head a smidgen higher, an extra bounce in her step. She carried herself like a queen. *That's what we'll do next.*

"Where to now?" Michelle's voice shimmered with excitement for whatever adventure awaited her.

He shook his head. "Can't tell. It's a secret."

"Oooh, I like secrets." And she seemed to mean it.

They didn't reach his destination as soon as he had hoped. As they strolled toward the opposite end of the festival, they passed importuning artists who made Joe promise to return another day to look at their work. Michelle directed people interested in face painting to Gil's stall. They stopped for more lemon ice to ward off the heat. At last brightly colored awnings came into view, and Joe steered her toward the CHILDREN'S ART ZONE sign.

"Children's art?" Doubt crept into her voice. "But we're not—"

"Children? They don't care. Anyone who wants to can experience art hands-on. Last year I helped paint one of the local buses, a paint-by-numbers kind of thing. It's fun."

Several different tables held materials from plain paper to wood and nails to wire. Joe found an empty corner at the wire table. He selected strands of purple, yellow, red, and blue, but as he twisted the wire, he felt Michelle's warm breath on his neck, her hands resting on his shoulder.

"You're making me nervous," he said good-naturedly. "Sit down." The child next to him had finished his piece, a circular contraption that looked remotely like an igloo, leaving a chair empty for the moment.

"No thanks." Michelle dropped her hands from his shoulder. "Wire's not for me. I have a hard time knotting thread with a needle. I think I'll stick with construction paper, over there."

"Tell you what. I'll make something for you, and you make something for me."

Michelle studied the bundle of wires in front of Joe, wrinkling her nose as if imagining what he might create. "Let's do it."

Joe studied Michelle's departing back, admiring its straight lines and mentally measuring the circumference of her head at the same time. The wires he had so carefully gathered had disappeared, the rare purple one finding its way into a preschooler's pile. He started over again with four yellow bands, twisting and tying them together. Looking up from his work, he saw Michelle absorbed over her work, coaxing glue out of a bottle.

"How's it going?" he called.

She looked up as if startled at the intrusion of his voice. "Great. I'm having fun."

They finished their projects at the same time. Someone took Joe's chair before he lifted his masterpiece off the table. He met Michelle midway. Her right hand was tucked behind her back, her picture out of view.

"This is for you." Sunlight glinted off the blue, red, and green wires nesting interlaced with the yellow base. "A tiara for a beautiful princess." *Now I sound like Sir Cameron.* He smiled to himself.

"Is that how you see me? As a beautiful princess?"

To answer, he set the tiara on her head. He kissed her cheek and bowed at the waist. "Sir Cameron has vowed his fealty to her royal highness, Princess Michelle of the Cherry Creek Arts Festival."

"You have to explain about Sir Cameron."

"Blame my mother for that. She named me after a long-ago ancestor, Sir Cameron Innis."

"So your name is. . . ?"

"Cameron Joseph Knight." He rolled his shoulders. "But she soon figured out I was more of an ordinary Joe than a knight of the round table."

"Sonia doesn't think so. She called you Sir Cameron. You can't tell me she's only a business associate."

"It's. . .complicated."

"And it's really none of my business. Sorry I asked."

"No harm done." Joe shook his head. "Come on. Yours next."

"Now mine seems so ordinary."

"Let me be the judge of that."

Brightly colored shapes created a park scene. A yellow sun cheered the sky, and small pink flowers sat atop triangular green stems. Music notes danced over the head of a small boy.

"It's—interesting." He tapped his chin with his forefinger. "Is that supposed to be me?"

Michelle blushed. "You have such a playful spirit."

"Like a little boy who hasn't grown up yet?" Joe grinned.

Michelle's face turned pink in embarrassment. "Well, yes. And you love to surround yourself with beautiful things."

"I'd better watch out—you know me about as well as Gil does." The idea pleased him.

"Anyone who can be a knight and a clown at the same time is bound to be interesting." She giggled as she reached out and touched the end of his red nose.

"Are you saying I'm schizophrenic?" He made a funny face.

She laughed. "Multifaceted. It's a good thing."

A couple walked by, matching handmade stovepipe hats atop their heads. "Want to try that next?"

Michelle threw a startled glance in his direction but agreed. One by one she was shedding concealing layers, each new "skin" more attractive than the last. Joe anticipated discovering the core.

৵

I can't believe I'm doing this. Michelle stared at the paper grocery bag in front of her. She had folded and stapled the open edges, adjusting the opening to fit her head. Gold foil stars and red, blue, and white ribbons lay scattered on the table around her. She had chosen a patriotic theme in keeping with the Fourth of July.

Sounds of a high school band floated through the air from a nearby stage. From what she could hear, the musicians were playing a painful adaptation of The Beatles' classic "Strawberry Fields Forever." Better than some of what passed for music nowadays, she supposed. How well she remembered the arguments with her high school band director. He had wanted them to play Sousa classics like "Stars and Stripes Forever." As drum major, she argued for more contemporary music. He suggested a democratic process—one representative from each section of the band would help him choose music for the marching band. How seriously the committee had taken their work, and what an odd assortment of music they had chosen. They wound up marching to everything from Beethoven to Bacharach with a heavy dose of rock and roll.

The music set her feet to tapping, and her knee banged the table in time. She glanced at Joe and noticed he was waving a wire in time to the rhythm. "I used to play the bass drum." He matched his words with acting out banging either side of an invisible drum in front of him. She giggled.

"And I was the drum major." She lifted her hands in the air, directing a couple of measures in four-four time. She squirted more glue on the last gold star and let the hat dry for a few moments.

"May I use the glue?" a little girl with Chinese features asked. Michelle handed her the bottle, studying her dark hair and serious eyes, which reminded her of many children she had seen in Romania. The thought dampened a little of her enthusiasm. The children at the orphanage didn't have the opportunity to make funny hats. *Oh Lord, open the doors.*

She and Joe finished their hats at about the same time. His creation belonged in a circus. He had curled paper like confetti, and ribbon streamers floated down the sides like a circus tent. With a bow and a pretend honk of his red nose, he took off his cowboy hat and put it on. The bag covered half his forehead, coming to rest just above his eyebrows.

"Let me try something." Michelle placed the Stetson on the table and tugged the clown hat over the crown. "I think this will hold it in place. I could staple it to secure it."

He shook his head. "No staples on that leather, please."

Michelle held her hat out for inspection.

Joe studied her creation. "I like it. But it could use one last thing." He unearthed a tall white feather and stapled it to the front of the hat. "There." He eased it over her head and frowned. "But now you're missing your tiara." He took the hat off and gently put the tiara into place around the bottom of the bag. When he put it back on, he made sure it rested snugly behind her ears. "Now we're dressed to go out on the town. You ready for some jazz?"

They glided away from the table, high-stepping as if they were Ginger Rogers and Fred Astaire. She joined in the impromptu dance. Smiling people watched their progress.

Sweating under the heavy hat, Michelle felt her hair sticking to her scalp and longed for another cold drink. Up ahead she spotted a coffee shop. They must serve iced drinks in the heat. "Let's stop for a minute."

Joe opened the door for her. She reached for her hat, but Joe stopped her, pointing to other customers in the store. Several of them were wearing similar stovepipe hats, some handmade, some purchased. Among the customers she spotted the same little girl who had borrowed the glue. Her hat was decorated with a 3-D flower made out of a cupcake liner and green construction paper. Cute. Her mother's hair was blond, and Michelle realized the child must be adopted.

four

What am I doing here at this festival, as if nothing mattered more than having a good time? The girl looked at Michelle and giggled, pointing at her hat. Michelle touched her hat and made a face. The child giggled some more. They communicated without language, and once again Michelle thought of Romania. Then their drinks were ready, and she and Joe found seats. She removed the hat, keeping it out of the way of their glasses and the shortbread cookies Joe had purchased. Taking a bite of the cookie, she looked at the passing crowds, wondering how she was going to meet her commitments.

"What's wrong?" Joe's tone shifted from lighthearted humor to compassion. He stretched his muscled arms across the table, light from the nearby window glinting off the blondish-brown hairs.

She shrugged, embarrassed. "Nothing." *Not with you.* "I'm thinking about the résumés I sent out and wondering if I'll ever get a job in this economy."

Concern flickered in his cobalt blue eyes. "God will open the right doors."

"I know. Sometimes it gets to me, but I'll be okay." She looked at the plate, almost surprised she had finished the cookie. "Do you mind terribly if we call it a day?"

❧

Joe swallowed his disappointment. To get back to the truck, they had to walk the length of the blocks cordoned off for the festival. Michelle hummed quietly to herself, and Joe took heart. As they passed the jazz stage, she asked, "I'd like to stop for a minute. Is that okay?"

Joe would have agreed to almost anything to prolong his visit with Michelle. They took a couple of seats toward the back, and when Joe reached for her hand, Michelle let him. As the bass picked out the rhythm and a saxophone carried the melody, her fingers lost their stiffness, and he found himself rubbing his thumb along her palm. A glance at her feet revealed she had kicked off her high heels. Joe still didn't enjoy the music very much, but he did enjoy watching the woman by his side.

When the set ended and the band struck the stage to prepare for the next act, Michelle turned to him. "Thank you." She turned the hat she had made in her hands. With a small smile, she returned it to her head. "I might as well get back in the spirit of the holiday."

They continued making their way through the booths, and Michelle stopped long enough to buy the purse she had perused earlier. All too soon they arrived back at Joe's truck. He unlocked the door on the passenger side, but Michelle climbed in before he could offer his assistance. He shut the door for her and returned to the driver's seat. "Where do you wish to go, princess? Your wish is my command."

"The Romeros', please."

The truck started with a loud growl and idled through the stop-and-go traffic around Cherry Creek Mall. Michelle stared at the crowds through the side window. Her hat slid sideways, and she took it off. She fingered the tiara. "I wish I were a fairy-tale princess who could call on all the creatures of the forest to make everything right with the world." She glanced sideways at him. "Or that I had a knight in shining armor to do it for me."

They arrived at the Romeros' house. Michelle's hand was

already on the door handle.

"Wait." Joe jumped out and ran to her side.

"I'm not used to such chivalrous treatment."

"Camelot is alive and well." He grinned. "I'd like to have dinner with you tomorrow night." *Please say yes.*

Michelle's eyes probed his. "Are you sure you want to?" For a second, her defenses dropped.

"Absolutely."

"Very well." A hint of a smile lifted the corners of her mouth, and she disappeared inside the door.

વે

An hour later, Joe waited while Sonia undid several locks on her studio door. "I see you added extra protection."

"Several studios have been broken into lately. And with what happened. . .you know. . .it seemed like a good idea. Come in; look around."

Sonia had changed things since his last visit. Angels and cherubs stared at him from all four walls.

"Not quite your usual work." He bent forward to study a cherub watching over a sleeping child.

"No, but it sells. Even starving artists have to eat." She tucked her arms around her waist for dramatic effect.

"Huh." He stopped to study her pose.

She waved him away. "Keep looking."

Sonia specialized in her use of bold primary colors, marrying the simplicity of a children's picture book with themes that resonated into adulthood. In her newest pictures, he sensed someone watching over the angels as they watched over their charges. God, of course. His heart quieted as he contemplated the involvement of the Heavenly Father in every aspect of life. He shook his head.

"You don't like them?" Sonia frowned. "I thought you would see what I was trying to do."

"It's not that." He mentally shook off the cobwebs of the afternoon and concentrated on the business at hand. "You don't need me to tell you they're good."

"Compliments are always welcome."

"They're a powerful testimony to God's intimate involvement in His creation. I can't take them all, but—"

"Great. We'll settle the details later." Tension flooded out of Sonia, almost drowning Joe in its release. "Since I've been painting angels, I baked an angel food cake. Care to have a slice? With strawberries, to celebrate our continuing association?"

Joe waited while Sonia fixed fresh-ground coffee and served a thick slice of cake dripping with fresh strawberries. One bite, and he closed his eyes as the flavor sensations flooded his mouth. As perfect as he remembered. The cake slid down his throat, and he quickly emptied the plate.

Sonia laughed. "There's plenty more where that came from." Without asking, she slid another slice onto his plate.

He smiled his thanks, sopping the cake in the strawberry juice. Sonia left a bit of her tiny piece. *Women, always worried about their weight.* Dabbing at the corner of his mouth with a napkin, he pushed away from the table. "Thanks."

"My pleasure, Sir Cameron." Sonia liked to tease him about his knightly dreams. She nodded her head as if pleased with what she had accomplished. "There's something else I want to show you. Something I'm working on."

Joe followed her into her inner room. A sturdy easel supported a large canvas. Jagged mountains, tall and unassailable, divided the picture in two halves. Black shadows cast a pall over a band of travelers seeking a way to the other side. A garden of paradise's delights awaited them there, surely the goal of the explorers.

Sonia's hand reached for the light in the painting, her

fingers stopping millimeters away from touching the surface. "I know you blame yourself for what happened that night. I blamed myself, too."

"It wasn't your fault—"

"Stop it." She put her fingers to his mouth. "I went to a counselor at my church. She suggested I paint how I felt about what happened. So I started this. Every time when I felt scared about going back to that part of town, or whenever guilt attacked me for my part in putting us in danger, I would paint the shadows a little darker, the mountains a little taller. I couldn't figure out how to get to the other side until recently. Then I found the way. Do you see it?"

Joe cocked his head and scanned the painting inch by inch. Sonia's brush had blocked all passes over the mountains. Tucked away in a deep crevice between the two tallest mountains was a fissure of light, a light so pure that the source must be God Himself.

Sonia saw he had found it. "God showed me He would guide me through my deepest fears instead of removing them from my path."

Joe only shook his head. He had never reconciled what had happened with the powerful God of scripture.

Sonia didn't press her point. "I want you to handle this for me when it's finished. I'm in no hurry to sell it. Hold on to it long enough to absorb the sense of peace God has given me." She laughed lightly, as if embarrassed at her suggestion that the painting could help him.

"We'll see." Joe didn't relish a visible reminder of an episode he was trying to put behind him.

Sonia nodded and turned off the lights as they exited the room. "More coffee?"

"No thanks."

"I have something for you before you go." Sonia disappeared

into her studio and reappeared with one of her angel paintings, a cherub watching over a child watering a flower. "I want your mother to have this one."

Joe thought about the gardens at his mother's house. "She'll like it. Thanks." He chose a handful of angel pictures for his gallery and left.

All the way to the hotel, Sonia's and Michelle's voices argued in his head. They both needed someone strong, a man of faith, a knight, indeed, and he was little more than a bungling squire.

❧

"The sun must have been strong today." Carrie rubbed aloe vera lotion onto Michelle's sunburned skin. "Maybe you need a higher SPF at this altitude."

Michelle knew Carrie was curious about the day, but somehow she didn't want to share the special memories. Not yet. Carrie didn't push. "Should I plan on your being here for dinner and fireworks tomorrow, or have you made plans with Joe?"

Dinner. Michelle had forgotten tomorrow was the holiday when she promised to go out with Joe. Maybe she should beg off. "I'm not sure. Can I let you know later?"

"Of course." Carrie paused at the door. "I'm looking forward to hearing all about it, when you're ready."

Michelle stretched out on the bed, reviewing the day. She had a lot of fun with Joe, but was it fair to go into a relationship when her future was so uncertain? "Oh Lord, You're going to have to help me. Not that I was ever in control. You are."

five

Joe combed his hair, a tuneless whistle streaming through his teeth. Excitement bubbled out in song for him. He couldn't wait to see Michelle again. In spite of the way yesterday had ended, she intrigued him more than any woman he had met for a long time. No woman in his hometown came close. Between the excitement of the holiday and the anticipation of seeing Michelle again, he had struggled to keep his mind on business all day.

His hand hovered over his suit, and he debated whether to dress up or stay casual. Casual, he decided. Somehow barbecue and fireworks clashed with the attire of a debonair businessman. He wanted to set the right tone tonight, to avoid the crowd-crushing scenes of the baseball game and the arts festival and find a place where he could learn more about this vulnerable woman who fascinated him so much. Dinner at a quiet restaurant, maybe followed by fireworks— that was the ticket for the evening.

When Carrie answered the door, a questioning look on her face, his spirits plummeted. "Michelle will be ready in a few minutes. Why don't you take a seat in the living room?" She disappeared up the stairs.

Joe shrugged and walked past a grand piano to the couch.

"Hi there. Joe Knight, isn't it?" A dark-haired man extended a hand in welcome.

"Mr. Romero, good to see you again." Joe shook his hand then sat on the couch to wait.

"It's Steve. And this is Viktor." The father ruffled his son's dark curls. "We're playing a close game of Candyland. He won last time, but I hope to even the score this time."

Joe watched the matching dark curly heads bent over the board. Steve groaned when he hit Molasses Swamp. "Just when I was ahead." Then Viktor landed on a shortcut and sped to the finish.

With a start Joe remembered the child was adopted from the orphanage his church helped support. He certainly looked like he was born to the Romeros. A child. Someday, maybe. When he found the right woman.

"Do you want to play?" Viktor asked.

"Please, join us. Maybe I can beat you." Steve flashed a smile at him.

Beyond the door he heard the murmur of women's voices, interspersed with giggles. Apparently Michelle wasn't ready yet.

Joe had made it halfway around the board and slid back behind the others when at last Michelle came in. No makeup today, her hair pulled back in a ponytail, and wearing jeans, she looked as beautiful as ever to him. He stood and bussed her cheek. "It's good to see you again." Somehow he knew tonight was important.

"I'm sorry I took so long." She looked away for a moment. "I couldn't decide whether to cancel tonight or not." Her cheeks reddened, and he felt an answering heat flare in his face.

"The thing is, I had made plans with the Romeros for tonight."

"Then I convinced her we could survive without her for the night." Carrie grinned. "Go ahead." She steered Michelle in Joe's direction.

Steve's gaze flickered between Michelle and Joe. "I guess we'll be seeing you later. Have a good time."

"So I'm ready if you are." Michelle's lips turned up in a smile.

"But Auntie Michelle, I thought you were going to the fireworks with us." Only Viktor seemed surprised at the change of plans.

"Not tonight, sweetheart." She bent down to kiss his dark head. "I'll see you tomorrow."

They walked to the truck without speaking, and she swung easily onto the passenger's seat. Joe turned the key in the ignition but didn't drive. "We could do this another time if you'd rather." Although he didn't know when. He needed to get back to Ulysses soon.

"No." Michelle's laugh sounded a little self-conscious. "I'm looking forward to tonight. Really."

Joe tapped the steering wheel. "What appeals to you? Dinner at a restaurant or a picnic on a mountaintop?"

"No contest. The picnic on the mountain."

When they got on the road, Joe flipped the air conditioner switch, but no air flowed out. "Looks like the air conditioner's on the blink."

Michelle had already rolled down her window and nestled her head in the crevice by the seat, the wind whipping her ponytail like confetti streamers. The truck shot onto the interstate.

"Where are we going?" Michelle projected her voice over the roar of air blowing through the cab.

Joe looked where the fast-approaching foothills paradoxically shut out the view of the highest peaks. One thing he did miss about Denver was the constant view of the mountains. Ulysses sat in the middle of the prairie, not quite a hundred miles from the first glimpse of the Rockies. "Have you been to Lookout Mountain yet?"

She shook her head. "Haven't been in the mountains at all."

Good. He relished the opportunity to be first to share one of Denver's greatest attractions with her. They approached the ascent up the mountain, past familiar landmarks: the Mother Mary Cabrini Shrine and the rich town of Genesee that for some reason always made him think of the book of Genesis in the Bible. Soon they reached their exit.

"Buffalo Bill Cody is buried up here," Joe told Michelle. Away from the speed and noise of the highway, they could hear each other. He had driven the road often enough that he almost knew the twists by heart. Mountain splendor alternated with panoramic views of the plains.

"He was that guy with the enormous yellow mustache, right? The original stage cowboy?"

"Before that, he was the real thing. Rode scout with the army, hunted buffalo, the whole bit. He started his Wild West show to keep the tradition alive."

For the next hour they poked through the Buffalo Bill Museum. Michelle read every word of the plaques. Dusk was darkening the sky as they sat at a table near the gravesite, enjoying the view and munching on their food.

"I wonder what it looked like down there back then," Michelle said.

"I expect it was a lot like where I live. Flat land dotted with trees and animals. Although Denver was a city, even then." He jumped off the rock where he was sitting. "Come on, I want us to watch the sunset over the mountains. And this should be a good place to watch the Denver fireworks, too. High enough to see them across the city."

Joe led Michelle to his favorite westward-lookout point. Row upon row of mountains stretched back into a purple haze. The fireball of the sun burned away the last remnants of day in a turquoise blue sky. He drew in a deep breath of the crisp, clear air. Silence reigned in the mountains, wind rustling through the trees, birds calling, but none of the noises of the city. He prayed the scene would work its magic with Michelle.

She sprawled beside him on a broad rock, long legs dangling over the edge, bare toes tipping in the sand and grass underfoot. A gentle rain sprinkled a few drops, and she lifted her arms as if welcoming the moisture. " 'I lift up my eyes to the mountains—where does my help come from? My help comes from the Lord, the Maker of heaven and earth.' That verse takes on a whole new meaning up here."

"Whenever I need a refresher course about how small I am and how big God is, I head for the hills." In fact, he had spent a weekend backpacking through the mountains before he'd decided to return to Ulysses.

"I know what you mean."

Joe lifted an eyebrow. "Didn't know there were mountains in Illinois."

"You'd be surprised. Actually, I was thinking of Romania. We had a couple of retreats in the Carpathian Mountains. It helped to get away from the pressure of our work for a few days."

"Did you enjoy your time in Romania?" Joe prompted when she stopped speaking.

"Oh yes. The need was so great. I felt like I was making a real difference."

"What did you do?"

"Outreach and evangelism—I led a Bible study for women, and we saw every one of them come to Christ."

"Praise God."

The sun disappeared from view, leaving them in darkness.

"Do you ever think about going back?" Joe held his breath. Someone committed to missions overseas would have no interest in an art dealer.

She shrugged and sighed. "No. That part of my life is over. But. . ."

"Yes?"

"I've promised to support the work. If I'm going to live in the lap of luxury—sorry, that's how I see the United States sometimes after being in Romania—it seems like the least I can do. And I'm paying on college loans. My parents paid on my loans while I was in Romania—they said it was their part of supporting my work—but then Dad lost his job, and it's been hard for them. I want to give them that money back."

He whistled. "That's a lot to manage all at once."

"I was doing okay, as long as I had a job."

"What happened?"

"The company downsized." She frowned. "And I've had trouble landing another position that pays enough for my commitments."

He reached for her hand in the dark and covered her fingers with his, offering his support. "I'll pray God provides just the right job for you. Soon." They sat for a few moments, absorbed by the scene in front of them. Joe hummed a few measures then started to sing. "Let all mortal flesh keep silence, and with fear and trembling stand; ponder nothing earthly minded, for with blessing in His hand, Christ our God to earth descendeth, our full homage to demand."

He stopped singing, and silence reigned absolute. He worshipped in the open air and beauty of God's creation.

Beside him, Michelle trembled. "That's beautiful. I've never heard it before."

"It's an ancient song that made its way into one of my mother's hymnbooks. She thinks it may be a plainsong—you know, like one of those Gregorian chants monks used to sing."

"Christ descended to earth with blessing in His hand. I like that thought."

They turned east again, looking over the city lights before them. Joe drew Michelle against his shoulder. He wanted to help her, protect her, fight her battles, love her—

The thought hit him hard.

God, I love her.

I can't love Michelle. I've only known her a couple of days. Joe's mind reasoned with his heart without success. Joy sang through his body. His breath quickened, and he slipped his arms around her shoulders, wanting to protect her from all harm.

Michelle's breathing settled into the same rhythm with his heartbeat. In the distance, color burst into the velvet darkness.

six

Michelle relaxed, relishing the comfort of Joe's arms and letting go of her worries about the future and enjoying the moment. She shifted in his arms, catching a glimpse of the mountains stretching south of her. The mountains were still visible, black silhouettes against a dark sky. In this idyllic setting, she found it easy not to ponder earthly minded things.

A breeze caressed her, whispering peace to her heart. Joe's breath warmed her inside and out. For the moment she relaxed, resting in the awareness of God's presence, thanks to Joe. He knew how to bring out the best in her. She felt like she had known him for years, not a matter of days. *But he'll be leaving soon. He's only in Denver on business. He has to go home sometime.*

The thought panicked her, and she sat upright, leaving the safety of his arms. "How long will you be in Denver?" She bent over and put her socks and shoes back on.

"I'm not sure." Joe stood up slowly, as if stretching kinks out of his legs. His voice sounded ragged, torn by some strong emotion. "I had planned on going home tomorrow, but. . ."

Will I see you again?

"I have some unfinished business. Maybe I'll stay another week."

Michelle's heart soared. She stood beside him, tingling from the buzz that sped from her head to her sleeping legs.

He glanced at his watch. "Wow. It's after ten."

"I'd better get back. Now that the holiday is over, I'm going job hunting in the morning."

Joe kissed her fingers then cradled her hand in his as they walked to the truck. The gentle pressure sent a message of strength and support. He opened the door for her and leaned against the frame. "When can I see you again?" His voice was light, but it throbbed with an unspoken deeper emotion.

Michelle warmed to the sound. "I really need to do some job hunting tomorrow. Thursday maybe?"

"Thursday it is, then." His face scrunched in a happy smile as if he were calculating the number of hours until then.

The Romero household had gone to bed when Michelle returned. Carrie had left a note. "Hope you had a good time. See you in the a.m."

A pang of guilt jabbed Michelle. Carrie was taking off the summer between finishing her Master's degree in May and sending her son to school for the first time in the fall. The two friends had looked forward to spending time together—at least until Michelle met Joe. Bless Carrie, she didn't seem to mind. If anything, she was delighted, but Michelle hoped to make up for the neglect. She went through her bedtime routine, pushing thoughts of the evening with Joe into the background, focusing instead on the tasks that lay ahead.

ஐ

Keep your mind on business, Joe reminded himself for about the hundredth time. He had tarried too long at the wood-carver's booth, entranced by the many figurines of couples. Old couples, young couples, expectant couples, even young children. *Everything reminds me of Michelle*, he admitted to himself. He had to make a decision if he wanted to visit all the booths before the festival ended later today. "So, Roger, have you had a successful time this year?"

The artist, a gray-bearded man of fifty-something, shrugged. Sometimes the entry fee exceeded the profits for the artisans, the major benefit coming from the exposure they received. Joe thought a few of Roger's pieces had sold, but he didn't trust his memory about anything that happened Monday—the day Michelle stood at his elbow, distracting every thought.

Joe quickly chose a fiftieth anniversary piece, a bride and groom, and the expectant pair. Roger shrugged, perhaps a little disappointed at not making a bigger sale. Flushed with full-blown romantic feelings, Joe relented. "If these sell quickly, I'd like some more. Are you willing to lower the price at all?" Although the figurines were lovely, he knew most buyers would balk at the high price tag.

Roger caressed a carving with his hands, probably remembering the countless hours required to bring it to life. "If you think it's necessary. What do you suggest?" They arranged a more attractive price. "Minus your commission, I suppose?"

Joe simply smiled. They shook hands on the deal and made arrangements for shipment. After that he moved swiftly from booth to booth, conducting business. Shortly after noon, the strains of karaoke grew stronger as he approached the country-western stage. He stopped for a second to watch.

A young couple in their early twenties pranced around the stage, singing an old Garth Brooks song. "We're two of a kind, workin' on a full house."

He smiled at the memory of the good time he and Michelle had shared performing on that stage. Not that either one of them could sing well enough to win a contest, but it hadn't mattered. Her natural warmth and enthusiasm drew people in.

Michelle. He could sink in the depths of her sea-green eyes, glimmers of a beautiful soul within. Tomorrow couldn't come soon enough for him. Resolutely he pushed the thoughts aside to concentrate on the business at hand.

❧

On Wednesday, Michelle stayed too busy with job hunting

to think much about Joe, but as the afternoon drew to an end, she kept glancing at the clock, as if she could make morning come more quickly. She was studying her wardrobe, contemplating what to wear on her next date with Joe, when she heard the phone ring in the other room.

Carrie rushed to her door. "It's for you—Mercury Communications."

Mercury? Michelle didn't think she stood a chance with Denver's third largest communications company. Her head spun as she took the receiver.

"This is Michelle Morris." Good, she kept a clear, professional tone.

"This is Chavonne Walker from Mercury Communications. I've reviewed your résumé. I'd like to schedule an interview with you on Friday, if possible."

"I'd love to." Michelle struggled to keep her voice even. "When do you want me to come in?"

They set the time for ten a.m.

"You have an interview?" Carrie inquired eagerly.

Michelle nodded.

"Praise God."

Michelle grinned and skipped a short step. " 'My God will meet all your needs.' Oh Carrie, it's starting. I just know it is."

The phone rang again. Carrie answered then grinned. "She's right here." She handed the phone to Michelle. "It's Joe."

"Hello." She sounded as breathless as a person accepting an award.

"Hey, you don't have to get all excited. It's only me," Joe teased.

"Mercury Communications just called."

"That's cause for us to celebrate."

He said us. The implied closeness warmed Michelle's

already-giddy spirits. "It's just a job interview." She down-played it, striving for a casual tone.

"It's a foot in the door." He sounded hesitant.

"What is it?"

"Some people I know that worked there loved it. But others. . .well, they left before long."

"I need this job, Joe."

"I'm sure you'll be fine. Everything is better with Michelle Morris in it." He made it fit the jingle for Blue Bonnet margarine.

She giggled. "So, what's up?"

"I wanted to hear your voice."

She smiled. "Well, now you have."

"I wanted to make sure we're still on for tomorrow."

"Absolutely." Michelle might have promised to go to the moon if he suggested it, as excited as she felt.

"Ask Steve and Carrie if they mind if we hang out there for a few hours."

"What—?"

"You said you liked secrets."

"I'll wait if I must." She covered the receiver with her hand. "He wants to know if we can spend a few hours here tomorrow."

"Of course," Carrie said.

"See you tomorrow, then." The morning seemed very far away.

৯

Michelle woke early on Thursday, wondering what Joe had in mind for the day. When he arrived midmorning, he held a large bundle under his arm and carried a bag with his other hand. She opened the door for him. "Come on in."

Joe set down the parcels and returned to his truck for another bag.

"Would you like some coffee?" Carrie asked when he came back in.

"Sure. That sounds good. Do you have a table where we can work for a while? And can we borrow your son?"

"Sure. Would the coffee table in the den work?" Joe nodded, and Carrie poured coffee for all of them then led the way to the den. "Viktor, come here, please."

Joe was already pulling packages of various sizes out of his bag. "We're doing some product testing today. Hope you don't mind."

Michelle stared at the assortment of paper and paints and other art supplies spread across the tabletop, reminiscent of the festival. "What's up?" She pasted on her best smile. "Why do you have all this stuff? More children's art?"

"Didn't I tell you? My store is part art gallery, part art supplies. I want to interest people in art any way I can. My kids' classes are always full; that's why I thought Viktor might like to help."

Viktor dashed into the room and skidded to a stop. "Here I am."

"Mr. Knight would like your help, Viktor." Carrie pushed him toward Joe.

"I need a strong boy."

"I'm strong." Viktor pounded his chest.

"Then you're just the one I'm looking for. I want you to help me test these supplies. What color do you like?" Joe opened a box of chalk, and Viktor chose the red stick. "Draw me a picture."

"Of what?"

"Whatever you like."

Viktor stuck his tongue out and pressed down on the chalk, drawing a house. The chalk broke in half, and his mouth turned down. "I'm sorry. I broke it."

"That's okay." Joe leaned close to Viktor and said in a stage whisper, "It happens to me all the time. It's the chalk's fault."

"Why don't you try these next?" Michelle sharpened a few colored pencils. Viktor chose red, blue, and yellow. Midway through coloring a blue roof the pencil lead broke.

"It's the pencil's fault," Viktor told Michelle.

"We can fix that." She handed him the pencil sharpener. He finished a picture of a red house with a blue roof and a yellow door. "I want to hang this on the refrigerator."

"Good idea." Carrie walked with him into the kitchen. She stuck her head back in. "Anybody want more coffee?"

"No," Michelle said.

"I'm going to start on cookies to bring to church on Sunday."

When Viktor came back out to the den, Joe handed him modeling clay. The boy rubbed it between his hands, working it into a long green snake.

"They say this project is quite popular." Joe pulled a photo album the size of a three-ring binder out of the bag then dropped a bunch of fabric and whatnots on top of it. "I don't see what the attraction of scrapbooks is. Why would somebody pay that much money when they can buy an ordinary photo album for a third of the price?"

Michelle hardly listened. Fingering the leather binding, she eyed the bright paisley print against the soft brown cover. "It's beautiful."

Joe cocked an eyebrow at her. "So you like it?"

"Oh yes. It would make a perfect gift. . .or a special family project. . .doesn't take any special talent. Just scissors and time and tape."

"But why package it? Wouldn't people rather make their own? It would be cheaper."

"Some people do." Joe obviously didn't understand the

appeal. "But I'd love something like this. It's easier than trying to pick up all the odds and ends I'd need. I want to do something with the hundreds of pictures stored on my camera cards—from Romania and from Carrie and Steve's wedding. This would get me organized."

"Take this one then. It's yours."

Michelle wanted to refuse, thinking of the expensive price tag, but something in Joe's face stopped her. Her fingers rubbed the leather as if it already belonged to her.

"There's a catch." His smile grew wider.

"Of course there is."

"I'd like to display a sample at my store. Can I borrow it for a month or two after you're finished?"

Put my life on display? Before Michelle could put her refusal into words, Joe tucked the materials back into the bag. "Do it. Convince me it will sell."

"Very well." Michelle smiled weakly.

Viktor's snake had fallen apart in the middle, and now he was putting together an animal of some kind. Michelle looked at the stacks of materials. "What else?"

"Who wants fresh cookies?" Carrie appeared in the doorway.

"I do!" Viktor dropped the clay on the table and ran to his mother.

"That's pretty much it, except for the finger paints."

"If you want to go on, I can supervise him while he tries those," Carrie said.

"Sure, if you think he'd like it."

"Are you kidding?" Carrie laughed. "He still gets a kick out of soap bubbles."

"Well, then. Maybe he'd like to assemble this model car."

Carrie wrinkled her nose when she saw the small box. "I'll let Steve help Viktor with that one. But thanks—they'll both love it."

After that Joe whisked Michelle away into a summer wonderland. For lunch they dined at a restaurant that had a wall-sized screen that took them through a day in the African jungle. They punted down Cherry Creek in a boat while their guide regaled them with stories of Denver's beginnings as a mining town. Last of all they toured the Tivoli Student Union, a converted brewery that looked like a castle out of a fairy tale against Colorado's trademark blue sky.

Much later Joe drove slowly back to Carrie's house, Michelle's head resting on his shoulder. Joe had a way of looking at her that made her feel as beautiful as Miss America and as fascinating as the latest pop star. What a special man. He seemed to like her from the inside out.

Feelings of contentment and peace swirled through her. The gentle humming of the truck's engine lured her to sleep. Her last conscious thought was, *I could love a man like that.*

seven

"Well, what do you think?" Carrie stepped back so that Michelle could look at herself in the mirror.

Not bad, Michelle decided, turning her face from side to side. The faint sunburn she had received on the Fourth had turned into a healthy tan. She'd hardly needed makeup. "It's good."

Carrie fixed a strand of hair here, a fold of the skirt there, but Michelle's mind was elsewhere. Somehow she had known she would look her best today—and she suspected the extra self-confidence came from her time with Joe. "If they don't want to hire you, it's their loss," he had said. Platitudes, perhaps, but he made her feel special.

"Want to tell me about it?" Carrie straightened the hem of Michelle's skirt. "You've been mooning around all morning, sighing like you're love struck."

Carrie had been Michelle's best friend too long to put her off. "I think I am. Love struck, I mean."

"Ahh." Carrie drew in a breath. "I thought so. Good."

"What do you mean, good? I'm here to find a job, not—"

"And we both were in Romania to spread the gospel, but that didn't keep you from dating while you were there."

"And you're the one who fell in love." Although Michelle meant it as a lighthearted comment, even she could hear the slight edge.

"Yeah, I did. I still can't believe how God brought Steve and Viktor and me together." Carrie smiled at the memory. "Whatever the reason, you're happy, and that should help you at the interview."

59

"As long as I can keep my mind on the questions." Adrenaline surged through Michelle's veins, boosting her self-confidence to almost ridiculous levels. She could do it, with God's help.

"Keep that confident smile, and you'll do fine." Carrie pointed to Michelle's reflection in the mirror. "I see a capable young woman. You're good with people. You're an experienced leader. You have the right training."

Michelle's chin rose a notch as Carrie rattled off her skills.

"And don't forget you're multilingual."

"I doubt if there is much need for Romanian in Denver." Michelle giggled.

"Don't forget your French. And you're picking up Spanish fast. You already know as much as I do."

Carrie was right. Michelle had an ear for languages, and learning another romance language presented almost no challenge at all. She had learned a lot of Spanish in only one month's time, bombarded as she was by the media and people around her.

"*Buena suerte*," Carrie said. "Good luck. Although with your skills, you won't need it." They smiled together as if on cue, leaving Michelle ready to conquer the world.

"And one last thought about Joe," Carrie added as if unable to stop herself. "Jobs come and go, and careers change, but the right man is 'till death do us part.' What's more important in the long run?"

That's true, Michelle realized with a start. *But I can't think about him now*. She put the finishing touches on her toilette and left.

She followed traditional job-hunting advice: leave nothing to chance. Reconnoiter ahead of time. Thanks to the scouting trip she'd made, she knew how to maneuver through downtown Denver's confusing one-way streets and where to park.

Leave early. Bring an extra pair of hose. She had heard horror stories of getting a run down the back of the leg or breaking a heel right before an interview. *Which is why I wear a simple pump, with a spare pair in the trunk of my car, of course.*

She arrived at the Mercury Communications building with half an hour to spare. The receptionist, a wispy-looking young woman whose name tag read SUSIE, greeted her warmly and handed her a lengthy application form.

Michelle had come prepared with names, addresses, and phone numbers for her job history and references, even though they already had her résumé. Had someone actually called Pastor Radu in Romania? She doubted it, but it looked impressive.

"Would you like some coffee?" Susie gestured toward a half-full pot.

Visions of coffee stains on the all-important application flickered in Michelle's mind. "No thanks." Instead, to ease the dryness of her throat, she sucked on a breath mint. After she completed the form, she studied the company portfolio left as the only reading material in the reception area. With the burgeoning Internet industry, Mercury had grown exponentially, gobbling up half a dozen competitors along the way. No stats were available for the current fiscal year, but the president promised continued growth.

With still five minutes to go, Michelle walked around the reception area, wanting to give the appearance of studying the artwork and not of nervous pacing.

"Miss Morris?" a friendly voice inquired.

She turned and swallowed her surprise at the speaker's appearance. With her slicked-back hair and black horn-rimmed glasses, she looked like she had escaped from the classroom. Only no schoolteacher had ever dressed so stylishly.

Michelle found her voice. "Yes, I'm Michelle Morris. And you must be—"

"Chavonne Walker." The woman extended a manicured hand and beamed a thousand-watt smile, the kind designed to put anyone instantly at ease. All vestiges of the schoolmarm vanished, and Michelle recognized Chavonne as a warmhearted professional.

"This way, please."

Michelle followed her hostess through a maze of corridors.

"This is all confusing at first, I know." Chavonne named each department in passing.

What's the difference between Information Technology, Web Technology, and Computer Technology, anyway?

Many of the employees looked like they were straight out of college. Chavonne herself couldn't be older than thirty. Michelle's résumé sparkled with experiences these young kids wouldn't have yet. *Maybe my lack of experience doesn't matter as much as I thought it did,* she realized with a lift of her heart.

The tour ended close to where they had started, and they went into Chavonne's office. Michelle registered details of the room's—and the owner's—personality as she refused another offer of coffee. Paper neatly stacked, a potted plant in the corner, family snapshots on the wall—the personal details confirmed what Michelle had already observed about Chavonne. She was personable, approachable, competent, and professional.

"Are those your girls?" Michelle remarked as an opening gambit.

"Yes. Annie is six, and Nettie is two." Chavonne pulled a folder out of the top drawer of her desk.

"My best friend's son just turned six." Michelle smiled at the memory of Viktor blowing out the birthday candles. A pang struck her heart. She had no pictures of children to hang on her wall. *No husband either.* Another, deeper, pang.

Chavonne did not inquire about Michelle's family.

Children fell into the "don't ask, don't tell" category for potential employers.

Both women seated themselves, and the interview began in earnest. They dwelt at some length on Michelle's time in Romania. "You were with a mission board?"

Michelle couldn't read anything into her neutral tone, but she refused to apologize for her faith. "Yes, sponsored by my denomination."

Chavonne flicked away an imaginary dust ball. "I dreamed of doing that back in high school. Before my girls were born."

Was she a Christian, then? "You still can someday, if you want to. Several of the volunteers were older people. Sometimes an entire family goes to the field to help out for a week or two."

"Maybe." With a smile Chavonne turned the discussion back to Michelle. "So do you speak Romanian?"

"Oh yes. French, too. And here in Denver I'm working on Spanish."

Chavonne leaned back in her chair. "Excellent. What do you consider to be your strengths?"

This was Michelle's favorite part of any job interview—a legitimate reason to brag about herself. She mentioned her computer skills, foreign languages, leadership traits, her experience working with people in a variety of situations. "I've worked with the public since I was a little girl, helping in my dad's store."

Chavonne smiled. "And your weaknesses?"

Bingo. "I can get too caught up in details and forget about the bigger picture." She hurried to turn it into a strength. After all, weaknesses were only strengths turned around. "I'm very good at organization and prioritizing my work."

Chavonne patted down a stray hair and rose from her chair.

"I'd like you to meet Mr. Spencer, who handles employee training."

Meeting another supervisor—a good sign. Michelle matched Chavonne's quick pace down the hall.

"While you two talk, I'll go ahead to Bible study. A group of us meets once a week, during our lunch break. Oh, here's Jim."

Bible study? Michelle was thrilled to learn about an organized group of Christians in the company.

Mr. Spencer was a tall man with wire-framed glasses and a neon yellow bright shirt with a conservative black tie. He sat scowling at his computer screen, but a smile broke out when he saw Chavonne.

"Jim, I'd like you to meet Michelle Morris. She is here about our human resources position."

"Glad to meet you."

Chavonne slipped away. Jim covered much of the same ground Chavonne had, describing the responsibilities for the position she had applied for. "I'm in charge of training, but frankly, the way we've been growing, we need more help. I'm glad you're here." He grinned.

The hour had reached noon, and Michelle's stomach churned. She regretted the breakfast she had skimped on due to nerves.

"—would you like to join us for lunch?"

Had Jim read her mind? She looked guilty, she knew she did, with the warmth flooding her cheeks.

"I'd like for you to meet some of the others in our department." He steered her to the cafeteria.

Two hours later she had shaken hands with at least two dozen people and completed the required I-9 form. She took out her cell phone and punched in Carrie's number.

"Guess what? They want me to start on Monday."

eight

Joe packaged up the last of the paintings and handed them to the UPS clerk. He had ended up buying so many pieces he couldn't carry them all in his truck. *And where will I put them in my store?* He needed to get home and start making money again, not spending it. But not yet. He wanted to let Michelle know how he felt about her, but he was as shy as a schoolboy on his first date.

A ragged poster fluttered against the wall, and a robust King Henry VIII winked at him while he chowed down on a gigantic turkey leg. Joe recognized the advertising for the Renaissance Festival held in Larkspur, a town south of Denver, every summer weekend.

A picture flashed into his mind—Michelle with a circle of flowers on her head, her long gown sweeping the ground, himself in breeches and a doublet, down on one knee kissing her gloved hand.

That's where he would take Michelle next: the Renaissance Festival. She'd love it.

ஐ

"Unhand the lady, you yellow cur," a raucous voice called from high ramparts overhead.

Joe looked up and saw several men dressed in velvet doublets. He waved his arms as if to say, "You mean me?"

One of the men leaned farther over the edge of the rampart. "Sir, if you dare enter through the gate, I challenge you for the fair lady."

Another face appeared beside his.

"Prospero, you couldn't beat a turtle in a three-legged race. Fair lady, sir knight, enter the kingdom of Larkspur under the protection of his majesty, King Henry."

Joe glanced at Michelle, and she smiled. The medieval mood commenced outside the gates to the Renaissance Festival. Street performers vied for a few coins. A fake knight rocked back and forth on a two-legged horse, and jugglers added one colored ball at a time to their display. Bow and arrow tied to his back, a man introduced himself as Robin of Locksley and offered his protection from unwanted attention. Michelle tucked her hand around Joe's arm and prepared to enter the make-believe kingdom.

A dozen things competed for his attention at the same time—charming British accents, the ringing of a blacksmith's hammer, the scent of food sizzling over an open fire, the sight of clothing in color and texture not seen in contemporary life. As always, he felt he had stepped over a threshold into another world.

"My chariot caught fire—"

Joe caught the end of a conversation between two of the actors. *His chariot? Does he mean his car?*

He hurried, tugging Michelle in the direction of a dress shop that displayed finery of every kind, from dresses in brocade and silk to lace shawls to tall, black lace-up boots. A sign hanging over the door said BELLE'S SHOPPE.

"Milord, milady. Thank you for gracing my shop." The owner, presumably Belle, a tall woman in a plain cotton gown, greeted them warmly.

Joe gestured to Michelle. "What do you have that would be worthy of my lady Michelle?"

Michelle's mouth dropped open while Belle rustled through the gowns hanging in her shop.

Joe whispered a few words in the clerk's ear. "I'll be back." He disappeared out the door.

ॐ

He left me here?

Before Michelle could follow, the shopkeeper blocked the entrance, holding up a pale blue silk gown with a dropped waist for Michelle's inspection. "What do you think?"

"I'm sorry, I'm not interested." Michelle tried to move.

"Your knight was most insistent. A complete outfit for his lady. Now if you don't like the blue, perhaps you would like a wine brocade?"

Sensing she wouldn't escape easily, Michelle gave herself over to enjoying the variety of fabrics and styles offered in the shop. *They must cost a small fortune, even as a rental.*

At length the shopkeeper produced a dress that caused Michelle to catch her breath. A pale green bodice dipped into a forest green velvet skirt—perfect.

"There is a change room, if you would like to see how it fits."

Michelle caught sight of the price tag. She couldn't, wouldn't, let Joe spend that kind of money. . . .

"Any luck?" a familiar voice called from the door. Familiar until she saw him. That tall man with brown leather breeches hugging his legs and a midnight blue doublet emphasizing his well-muscled chest couldn't be Joe. Then his deep blue eyes peered out from under a feathered cap, and Michelle smiled from deep down inside.

"Oh Joe, you look fantastic."

"Milady Michelle was about to try on this gown." Belle gestured meaningfully with the garment in her arms.

Michelle heard Joe suck in his breath, as if imagining her in the garment. She wanted—needed—to wear the gown, if only to be worthy of his finery.

"I'll try it." She slipped into the side room, where Belle assisted her with the multitude of fastenings down her back.

The gown fit the lines of her body perfectly, emphasizing her good points and hiding her flaws.

"You are beautiful." Belle sighed in appreciation. "But perhaps one more thing?" The clerk disappeared through the curtains.

She returned with a snood in her hands, made with fine white lace, and fit it over the back of Michelle's head. Without the weight of her hair down her back, Michelle felt surprisingly cool.

"As for shoes..."

Michelle studied her feet, glad she had chosen sandals instead of gym shoes. "I'll be fine." Somewhat shyly, she stepped outside the curtain where Joe waited.

For a long moment, they looked at each other without speaking. Then slowly, almost reverently, Joe removed his hat and bowed to his knee.

"My lady." He reached for her hand, and his lips grazed the tips of her fingers. Slowly he rose, not once removing his gaze from her. His expression said she was the most precious thing in the world.

Michelle wanted to say, "It's just me; I'm not worthy." What came out instead was, "I can't let you rent this." To her ears, her objection sounded only halfhearted.

"I think the lady protests too much." Clasping Michelle's hand in his, Joe raised it to his chin and pulled her closer to him. Staring into her eyes, he declared, "You must do me this honor. If only for today, let me play at being the brave knight Sir Cameron." He looked at her with such a mixture of boyish excitement and manly pride that her heart melted.

Slowly, she nodded.

He raised her hand to his lips and blew softly across her knuckles. The gentle warmth of his breath tickled unknown nerve endings, thrilling her to the soles of her feet until she almost swooned in his arms. When they stepped outside the tent, they left the twenty-first century behind with their clothes at a check stand located conveniently outside the shop.

Michelle wanted to hug him. "If you are Sir Cameron, I must be—"

"Lady Michelle. A beautiful name for a beautiful lady."

Heat swept across Michelle's face.

They wandered a few steps without noticing where they were headed when a tall man in a helmet and brandishing a spike barred their path. "Hold there. What is your business before the king's court?"

Directly in front of them a semicircle of twenty or so men and women in period dress held court. At the center sat a man with full beard and rounded chest, with a dark-haired beauty at his side. King Henry, as promised, with Anne Boleyn.

"Begging your pardon, sir, we meant no disrespect," Joe said. They stepped aside to enjoy the spectacle.

While they watched, horns sounded and the monarchs rose to their feet, starting a stately procession downhill.

"It must be time for the first joust." Joe checked his watch then offered his arm to Michelle, and they fell in behind the royal court.

A sudden thought struck her. "I thought Robin Hood lived during King Richard's time." Michelle reflected back to the encounter at the gate.

"Time has no meaning here." Joe waved aside the discrepancy. "They mix centuries of the Middle Ages and the Renaissance in equal measure."

They paused long enough to buy water bottles, a necessity in the heat. Then they joined the crowd gathering at the rectangular tourney field. King Henry and Queen Anne had already settled in a shaded pavilion on the far side.

A couple of jesters worked the crowd, preparing them for the upcoming joust. "Sir Roland is a lout. His colors are silver and black. When he makes a pass, boo him."

The second jester, merry in scarlet and orange, added, "Sir Jerome is a heroic knight. He will be wearing gold and blue. Cheer for him."

They practiced. "Sir Roland." Loud catcalls and hisses rose from the crowd.

"Sir Jerome." Enthusiastic cheers and an occasional yee-haw erupted in increasing waves.

Trumpets announced the arrival of the contestants to a satisfactory chorus of cheers and boos. The first jester explained the rules of the joust. "Points may be earned on each pass the contestant makes at the target. Each target demonstrates a necessary battle skill."

The contestants faced their horses to the king and queen. Anne leaned over the parapet. "For you, Sir Jerome." She tossed him a white handkerchief.

The crowd cheered as loudly as they might a winning home run. For this day, this game, Sir Jerome was their hero.

Sir Roland scowled. "Lady's favors never won in combat." His voice was magnified loud enough for the spectators to hear.

"No, but with such an inspiration, how can I fail?" Sir Jerome said.

The crowd cheered once again and then fell silent as the squires set two hoops chest-high for the target.

Both knights easily lanced the two rings, as well as the four set for the next pass.

The second challenge appeared much more difficult. They had to hit a round ball suspended on a rotating pole hard enough to swing it around, or it would knock them to the ground.

Sir Jerome raced around the field on his horse, a magnificent white stallion, but pulled up short. Gaining speed on the second lap, he lunged at the target, a perfect hit with sufficient strength. The ball swung harmlessly out of the way, and his horse galloped to safety.

Sir Roland didn't fare so well. The ball didn't complete the circle and instead struck him between his shoulders, throwing him from his horse. The crowd roared with laughter. Sir Roland stood, wiping dirt from a surprisingly handsome face. Silently Michelle rooted for him to get back on his horse, to try again. His eyes scanned the crowd, as if searching for someone.

"I think I need the favor of a lady myself." He held out his hands in a plea. "Who will honor this poor knight?" He walked around the field.

Michelle felt her smile widen at the spectacle. Whom would he pick? He stopped in front of her.

"You, my lady. May I have a token of your esteem?"

Michelle looked into his eyes, black as coal. "Me, Sir Roland?"

He nodded.

She searched her purse for something appropriate. Beside her, Joe stirred.

"She will not." His growl deepened into a roar. "The lady is with me."

ઓ

The crowd came to life at Joe's challenge, cheering for one side or the other. Joe couldn't believe the jealousy that surged through him, shaking his voice. The knight stared at him strangely.

Michelle came to his rescue. "Sir Roland, I cannot. Sir Cameron forbids it."

A laughing light brightened Sir Roland's eyes. "Sir Cameron,

I desist. Perhaps we shall meet again?" He said it with convincing menace.

"Oh Sir Roland?" A few yards away, another spectator leaned over the fence, waving a lacy handkerchief. "You may defend my honor." The crowd laughed with her.

Joe relaxed when the attention turned away from him and Michelle. The joust concluded with Sir Jerome soundly beating Sir Roland.

Michelle's cheeks burned bright as they strolled down the lane. "That was rather sweet, the way you defended my honor back there."

"So I didn't embarrass you?"

"Perhaps, for a second." She flashed a grin at him. "But then I thought of all the times I wished I had a Sir Cameron to defend me. There's a lot to be said for chivalry."

If only protecting someone in the real world was as easy as standing up to Sir Roland today. Were things really so much simpler in the Middle Ages? More direct, at least, face-to-face with your enemy; and all knights, regardless of their allegiance, adhered to the same code of honor.

Michelle was studying a daily schedule. "The next joust isn't until two o'clock. There's storytelling and puppets and bagpipe music—"

He heard it then, a low voice singing. "Let all mortal flesh keep silence." Joe caught the edge of a shadow with his peripheral vision and whirled around.

"Pardon me, sir." Less than a yard away a tonsured figure in a monk's robe crouched close to the ground, humming to himself. He twisted the rope tied around his waist between nervous hands. "Would you care to give an offering to the poor?"

"It would be my pleasure." Michelle's laugh rippled through the air, and she dropped a coin into the man's outstretched palm. "That song, it sounded familiar. What was it?"

"A snatch of plainsong, milady, such as we sing at the monastery." He smiled, a gap showing between two broken front teeth—probably a prosthetic device.

Joe remembered the street person she had aided the night they met. She was compassionate and generous, even at play, but this actor's behavior filled Joe with the same uneasy disgust as the shameless beggars on the 16th Street Mall. "You have your money. Begone then."

The beggar scuttled away as silently as he had approached. Joe let out a deep breath.

Michelle glanced at him sideways. "I saw the side of his bucket. There was a discreet web address for a rescue mission noted. I think it's legit."

Joe shrugged off his uneasiness. "There's a first for everything, I suppose. What next?"

"I can't decide. You've been here before. What would you suggest?"

"You might like the puppets—a variation on Punch and Judy—but if it's the same storyteller who's been here before, he's excellent at fractured fairy tales."

Michelle studied the schedule. "There's just about time for both, before the next joust."

A couple of men passed by, biting down on gigantic turkey legs. Joe's mouth watered.

"Yuck." Michelle's brow wrinkled as if in disgust.

No turkey legs today. A brave knight could endure long combat without sustenance. His stomach growled in protest.

"But it is lunchtime. What are our choices?" Michelle gazed around, searching for booths selling food.

In the end they settled for beef on a stick en route to the storyteller's tent. By the time they arrived, they found standing room only.

A thin man with a lively face underneath a tasseled hat

began speaking. "Once upon a time there was a feautibul lirg maned Rindercella who dilved with her neam metstother...."

Joe had heard it before, but once again wondered how the man managed a half-hour monologue in butchered language. At his side, Michelle first trembled with glee then reared back in laughter, the snood slipping off, letting her blond tresses fall in silken locks over her shoulders. Joe enjoyed watching her more than listening and soon lost track of the story.

How do I tell her how I feel? He couldn't ask for a more romantic setting than the Renaissance Festival, but Michelle seemed determined to wring every minute of pleasure out of it. So far they had run from one activity to another. He'd have to make an opportunity.

Soon the performer passed his hat, seeking donations. The businessman in Joe applauded the enterprising spirit, but the spectator resented being expected to pay even more money than the hefty entrance fee.

The afternoon passed swiftly. Joe thought he had his chance to speak from his heart when they sat alone in Da Vinci's Flying Machines, a man-powered ride. But Michelle craned her neck to see all the inventor's ideas and to exclaim over the strongly muscled men slowly pushing the cars around.

Toward dusk Joe led Michelle to a bench underneath a leafy tree. She plopped down, dropping her purse on the ground beside her. They sipped lemonade while Joe searched for the right opening. Her golden hair, once again tucked in the snood, gleamed silver in the setting sun. She took her sandals off and wriggled her toes in welcome freedom. She was so precious, everything he'd ever dreamed of and more.

"What a wonderful day. Thank you, Sir Cameron." She took a long drink of her lemonade and sighed contentedly.

Joe found himself sinking down on one knee. "My lady. My lady—"

A low humming buzzed in his ears. Before thoughts could form in Joe's mind, a hand slashed between them. Michelle's purse disappeared.

nine

Before Joe could rise to his feet, the monk blended into the crowd, shedding robe and wig as he sped away.

"Stop him!" Joe roared in a voice loud enough that several people stopped to see what caused the commotion. He sprinted after the thief down a thin path cleared by curious onlookers but saw no trace of the man he sought. Nearby he heard low singing, louder than before. He traced the source. A group of "monks" sang in unison on stage, but none of them looked familiar. The thief had gotten away.

"There you are," Michelle called from behind him. She sounded breathless.

"I lost him."

"I looked for his robe and wig but didn't find any trace of them. He must have taken them with him." Michelle sounded grim. "I doubt that money is ever going to make it to a rescue mission."

"No." Joe stood with his hands on his hips, turning in a slow circle, hoping to find some sign of the disappearing monk.

"We'd better tell someone what happened."

"I suppose." Joe put his arm around her shoulder, holding her close as they made their way back to the entrance where they found a burly man who looked like he could be King Henry's chief guard.

The chief of security scowled as they described what had happened.

"I'm ashamed to admit I gave him a few pennies earlier in the day. He pretended he was a beggar, you see." Michelle gave a description of the thief. "But I doubt I would recognize him, not without the costume." Her shoulders sagged.

"Is this the man?" The chief drew out pencil sketches of a man who captured the thief's look, toothy smile and all.

"Yes," Joe and Michelle answered together.

He grunted. "The singing monk strikes again. Our guards at the front gate have been alerted, of course, but our best guess is that he arrives in everyday clothes then changes after he arrives. He looks like anybody else the rest of the time."

"So you know who it is?" Joe asked. *Why haven't you caught him?*

"Unfortunately, no. But his MO is always the same. He stalks his victim sometime during the day. She hears a bit of humming, and then her purse is stolen. Otherwise, he is as stealthy as a shadow. The beggar is a new twist."

"I knew something about him didn't feel right. But Michelle said the sign indicated it was for the rescue mission. Sounded like it could be legit."

The chief frowned again. "We wouldn't allow something like that. Besides," he added with a trace of a smile, "I doubt there were rescue missions in King Henry's England."

Joe thanked the chief for his assistance. Michelle filled out the necessary paperwork and called her credit cards to cancel them. People were beginning to stream toward the exits. "Do you mind if we leave?"

"Of course not."

Joe hesitated for a moment outside of the clothing shop. "I wish I could get a picture of you in that dress."

She blushed. "Photography is a very *modern* invention."

He lifted her hand to his lips for one final kiss. "Then let me engrave the sight upon my eyelids." He held her eyes for a long moment before he slapped his forehead. "Of course. My phone." He dug it out of his pocket and snapped a picture before she could protest.

"Now it's my turn." She grabbed the phone and took his picture. "Perhaps Belle will take a picture of us together?" Belle was agreeable, and she snapped several shots before they exchanged their finery for their street clothes and headed for Joe's truck.

A few minutes later they were back on the road to Denver. Tension radiated from Joe's neck down his spine.

"Sir Cameron—"

"It's Joe. I'm no knight, not in the real world."

"Sir Cameron," Michelle repeated firmly. "Is there an inn nearby that will take two weary travelers such as ourselves?"

"There's a restaurant up ahead."

"Thanks." Michelle removed the snood and brushed her hair. "And Joe? You will always be my knight. Always."

Joe glanced at Michelle's pale face, dirt smudged on one cheek. What a horrible end to what he had hoped would be a very special day. At the restaurant's parking lot, he jumped out and rushed to get the door for Michelle. Weary as she was, she was beautiful in every way, a true lady. He held her hand as they walked into the restaurant.

"Did you folks come from the Festival?" The waitress's friendly banter burned like a brand on his spirits, and his stomach tightened. He had enjoyed the day until. . .

Michelle made some polite response and escaped for the lady's room as soon as they ordered their beverages. "What do you want?" Joe called after her.

She paused long enough to answer. "I'll get whatever you're having."

Neither one of them said much until midway through the juicy half-pound burgers the restaurant specialized in. The food sent messages along Joe's nerve endings like a drug, loosening the anxious knot in the pit of his stomach and relaxing his muscles. He finished his Dr Pepper in one big gulp. The waitress reappeared immediately with a refill.

Michelle squeezed lemon into her iced tea. "I can't believe what happened."

"Yeah." Joe bit off another chunk of his hamburger and chewed. After he swallowed, he said, "I want to be a knight, and instead I keep ending up like the court jester. Fooled by that stupid singing monk. I feel like I ought to be beheaded for incompetence."

"You heard what the chief said. It's happened before. This guy works the fair, and so far they haven't been able to catch him."

"Yeah, but sometimes it feels like trouble seeks me out." Drawing on his remaining dregs of courage, he dragged out the words. "It's happened before. One time I was out on a date—"

"With Sonia?"

He nodded. "And we were robbed—at gunpoint."

She reached out with her hand, silently encouraging him to continue.

"There were two robbers. One held a gun on us while the other one took our wallets, purses, jewelry—everything."

He jammed a few french fries in his mouth as if he could chase away the memories with food. "What's worse is that my parents were with us that night."

"What happened?"

"Dad already suffered from a weak heart, and the stress brought on a heart attack. He died not long after that."

"Oh wow. And you—"

"—went home to take care of Mom. Since I felt like it was my fault. My brother has his own family to take care of, and Mom needs help keeping up with everything." He sighed. "Sometimes I feel like God's fall guy."

"But God doesn't work that way."

"I know that. But—"

"But it doesn't always make much sense. Let me tell you a story. You know I met Carrie in Romania."

Joe nodded.

"And that Viktor came from an orphanage near Bucharest."

Again Joe nodded, wondering where she was headed with her story. "Our church supports the orphanage."

"Well, what you may not know is that it was a return trip for both Carrie and Steve. They went there the first time as part of a singing group."

"Oh?" *So what?*

"Steve was married at the time. To someone else."

Huh?

"And his wife was pregnant. She went into premature labor. She died, and the baby with her."

Joe's mind reeled. The cheerful man with the perfect family—Joe had envied him, he admitted it.

"I won't pretend to explain why God took Steve's first wife and child home so early, but I do know God gave him a beautiful new family. God never takes away something without giving us something even better." She laid down the last of her hamburger and looked him straight in the eye. "And neither you nor God sent the thief after us. The thief chose to do that all on his own."

"You're probably right." Joe twirled the straw through his Dr Pepper. "But after what happened today—again—I wonder if it's ever safe to open your heart to someone. People close to me end up getting hurt. And if there's anything I want right now, it's you, close to me." He took a deep breath and studied the glass. "You're the most wonderful thing that's happened to me in a long time, and I think I love you." There, he had said it. Blurted it out, in fact—nothing like the poetic phrases he had planned.

Michelle sank back against her seat as if stunned.

"But after what happened today—again—I wonder if that's a mistake. I can't afford to love somebody. Not if it means both of us getting hurt." Bitterness colored his words.

The waitress reappeared at their table. "Would you folks like dessert?"

ঌ

Michelle was grateful for the interruption. She gathered her thoughts while they ordered dessert before continuing the conversation. *I think I love you.* "Oh Joe."

"I know. I shouldn't have said anything, especially not after today."

"But Joe, I think I'm falling in love with you, too." She closed her hands over his, and for a moment the world stood still.

A warm flame flickered in Joe's eyes and then disappeared. "I refuse to be your bad luck charm." He withdrew his hand from hers and picked up the check.

"Don't be foolish. It could have happened to anyone."

"But it didn't. Not today." He clenched his jaw.

We're going over the same ground. Maybe we'll see things more clearly later. "When do you plan on going back to Ulysses?"

Joe blinked at the abrupt change of subject. "Tomorrow after church."

"Do you have any idea when you'll be back in Denver?"

"I usually wait several months between trips." He raised an eyebrow and grinned as if he couldn't help himself. "But I suspect I'll be back sooner this time."

The seriousness beneath their banter breathed life into Michelle's heart. *Is Joe the one for me, Lord?*

ঌ

Early Monday morning found Joe at his store, arranging his stock to show the new pieces to their best advantage.

He ran his fingers over the carving of the bride and groom. The bride was tall and willowy with long flowing hair—like Michelle. If only. He set the piece down with a sigh.

Should he have stayed and helped Michelle with all that was involved with replacing the contents of her purse? Not that he could do much except hold her hand. Business called him back to Ulysses, but his heart stayed behind in Denver.

Their parting words returned to him. "Will I see you when you come back to Denver?"

"Definitely." He couldn't stop the words.

"Make it soon." She had kissed him on the cheek before she darted inside Carrie's front door.

Already he was counting the days.

ten

Hardly any wind stirred. Joe lifted the Rockies baseball cap and wiped the sweat off his forehead. The weather was hot, as hot and dry as only July in Colorado could be. He grabbed a hot dog and took a swig from his water bottle. His niece waited her turn at bat during her Tuesday night softball game.

"Hey, batter, batter, batter," an overanxious mother called from the bleachers behind home plate. The girl tapped her bat on the ground, sending dust swirling into the air. Moments later she struck out and headed for the bench, head hung low. The mother leaned over the bench and whispered to her.

Pepper, his niece, came up to the plate.

"Choose a good one," his sister-in-law Judy called from beside him on the bleachers. They both cheered loudly when Pepper, a gangly seven-year-old redhead, managed a base hit.

Joe looped his legs over the seats in front of him and leaned back on his elbows. He breathed in the clean, fresh air, so much cleaner than Denver, and let out a contented sigh. "It's good to be back."

"It's good to have you back. Pepper's convinced they lost last week because you weren't here."

The next batter made contact with the ball, and Pepper slid into third base. The next two batters struck out, though, so she didn't score a run. Joe flashed Pepper a thumbs-up when she glanced at him from the bench.

"Did I miss anything?" Joe's older brother Brian slid onto

the bleachers beside them.

"Pepper got a base hit. They weren't able to get her home."

Brian shook his head in apparent disappointment. "I'm sorry I'm late. But Mrs. Feldkirk kept me talking for twenty minutes."

"That's okay. It's one of the things that makes you a good country doctor." Judy kissed him on the cheek. "I hope you don't mind that I locked up and came ahead."

"Of course not."

"At least your clinic is only five minutes away." Joe thought of the endless hours he spent driving from one end of Denver to the other, chasing down artists in their studios.

Conversation paused while Pepper scooped a ball out of the dirt and tagged the runner out at second base. Her team headed for the bench.

"I think I'll go say hello to my daughter." Brian stepped off the bleachers with one easy stride. Judy dug a bag of chocolate chip cookies out of her purse.

"Want one?" She passed Joe a handful, the chocolate melting and smearing all over his hands. "Sorry." She dug in her purse for a tissue.

Joe remembered the time Sir Roland had requested a token from Michelle. He missed her already. In fact, he had hardly stopped thinking about her.

Brian reappeared and grabbed a cookie. "So what kept you in Denver so long? We expected you back before the weekend."

Joe didn't want to talk about Michelle, not yet. His practical physician brother would scoff at the idea of falling in love with a woman he had known for only a week.

"Uh, some business came up that I had to attend to."

"Business with Sonia?" Judy grinned.

Uncomfortably close.

"Some, yes. She's working on a powerful new painting that she wants me to handle for her."

"And?" Judy prompted.

"And what?"

"And did you two get back together? You look like a cat who's feasted on cream."

"No." Joe shook his head emphatically. "That's all over with."

"Something happened."

"No, honestly, it didn't." *Not with Sonia at least.*

"Okay. You can have your secret for now." Judy turned her piercing eyes back to the game. Joe breathed a sigh of relief.

❧

Michelle read through her new employee handbook a second time. She had spent Monday in an orientation class for new employees, and Tuesday she was in training for her department, so today was her first day to work. She hoped someone gave her something to do soon. While she waited, she rearranged her workstation to her liking, stocked supplies, and sharpened pencils.

She stretched in her seat, stood up, and walked around. Notebooks that appeared to be training manuals stood on a low-lying bookshelf. She grabbed a couple and headed back to her desk. The first one, for Customer Service, outlined the rules of phone etiquette—smile in your voice, no one left on hold for longer than thirty seconds—familiar ground. Then it gave flow charts for answering customers' most common complaints. She had worked with that kind of material before and found it easy to use.

Material in the second notebook failed to impress her. Michelle returned both books to the shelf and glanced through the other volumes. Checking against the list of departments within the company, she found no material at all for a third of them. No wonder the turnover was high, a problem Chavonne had mentioned at her interview.

"Michelle. Glad I found you." Jim, the man she had met at her interview, paused in front of her desk.

She shook his hand. "Good to meet you again."

"Welcome aboard. We're having our departmental meeting in five minutes. I'll show you the way."

Minutes later they took the two remaining seats around a large oval table, surrounded by several faces Michelle remembered from her tour of the department. Their team consisted of an interesting mixture of races and gender, predominantly young. Chavonne sat at the head.

In the far corner a couple laughed. Michelle looked forward to developing the same camaraderie with her coworkers. That was the best part of any job. Their laughter grew louder. Michelle's heart lurched a bit. What would it feel like to be half of a couple sharing secret jokes that only the two of them knew about?

Chavonne called the meeting to order. She reeled off a list of things Michelle didn't yet understand, acronyms every company seemed to develop for their own way of doing business.

"—a warm welcome to our newest employee, Michelle Morris."

A few people applauded, and they went around the room introducing themselves. Michelle worked at associating something unique about each individual with his or her name, a skill she had honed to perfection with strange Romanian names. Remembering the women came easily, the men, less so. Rick had steel blue eyes, but none of the laughing merriment that shot warmth into Joe's sky blue irises. Gary wore an obvious toupee, nothing like Joe's glorious thatch of thick brown curls that made her fingers itch to run through it.

Why am I comparing every man to Joe? Michelle focused on what Chavonne was saying.

"Today we have the honor of being addressed by Glenda Harris, our senior vice president." From the covert grimaces exchanged around the room, Michelle guessed the VP wasn't well liked.

The door opened, and in strode a woman who emanated such authority that it took a minute for her petite size to register. From her carefully coiffured hair to her power suit, she demanded respect. Ms. Harris spoke about specific goals for employee training, with the aim of improving performance and reducing turnover throughout the company. She left little doubt that jobs were on the line—including Michelle's. She had to make an impact—fast.

❧

Joe turned the key in the lock, a simple dead bolt affair. Up and down Ulysses's main street, shopkeepers shut down for the night, turning off lights, rolling down blinds. Most stores now opened on Saturdays, but the mom-and-pop operations shut their doors at six on weeknights so that they could spend the evenings at home with their families. Even the chain grocery store closed at ten. At times Joe missed the twenty-four-hour convenience Denver offered.

Since his house was only a mile away, Joe often walked back and forth to work. Tonight he relished every step, re-acquainting himself with the minute changes a week had brought to his town. The mechanic had repainted his truck a bright red. Pictures of the candidates for Queen Penelope for the upcoming Odyssey Days had replaced wedding pictures in the portrait studio window.

He turned the corner. As so often happened, a pride of ownership surged through him. He had taken a ramshackle house and worked on it until it shone inside and out. He took special pleasure in the way he had xeriscaped the yard to allow for Colorado's semiarid weather.

Best of all, I don't even have to lock my house, Joe thought as he opened the front door. A black Labrador retriever skidded across the front hall and slid to a stop in front of Joe, his whole body wiggling with delight. Joe knelt down and cuffed his ears, offering his hands for a slobbery greeting. The dog's tail thumped the ground like a steam engine.

"Yeah, I see you, too, Gawain. Want some food?" The dog raced for the kitchen door at the words.

A package from Sonia had arrived in the mail. He set it to one side.

A quarter of an hour later, he plopped down in his easy chair with his microwaved pizza, Gawain lying beside him with his head between his paws. Joe flicked on the TV and took in the nightly news. The reporter told of a drive-by shooting in one of Denver's more well-to-do neighborhoods. More crime. He switched it off. If only they had a closer TV station than Denver. He activated the radio to discover the Rockies had played an afternoon game. The talk show held no interest for him, so he turned it back off.

He considered playing Frisbee with Gawain. One look out the front door nixed that idea. The fickle weather had turned into an early evening rain. He stood behind the screen door for a minute, enjoying the rush of moist, cool air. When the raindrops began filtering through the screen and beading the floor, he closed the door. The package from Sonia caught his attention. He carried it to his chair, slitting open the accompanying letter.

"Thought you might like this. . . . Don't forget me. I'm almost finished with my painting, and I hope you can handle it for me. . . . And isn't it time for a commission check?" She kept the tone businesslike and casual. Sonia had proven to be a true friend, even after they stopped dating. *I wonder what book she sent this time.* He carefully slit the wrapping with a knife.

On the shiny cover, flags fluttered in the breeze atop turrets over a medieval castle, a column of knights riding across an open drawbridge. The title piqued his interest, as Sonia had known it would: *Beyond Camelot: Other Legendary Knights.*

He flipped to the table of contents and found what he expected—a chapter about Sir Cameron. Flipping through the pages, he read the material. The author carefully defined what was known for certain and what was speculated about the little-known knight.

Sir Cameron had earned his fame by felling a hundred—a thousand in the more embellished versions—enemies, single-handedly protecting his lady's castle. A full-color illustration accompanied the story. Sword flashing, Sir Cameron stood in front of the castle gates. High atop the tallest turret, a tiny figure peered down on the battle.

How times had changed. Nowadays the lady would battle the villains by his side, and even together they might not succeed. He slammed the book shut. He could no more live up to Sir Cameron's chivalrous standard than he could walk on the moon. And people he cared for suffered for it. He still wondered if Dad would be alive today if he hadn't made the ill-fated trip to Denver.

❧

Michelle dug out the scrapbook kit Joe had left with her. *I promised.* And when she finished arranging the pictures, she would have a perfect excuse to contact him.

She slipped the first disk with pictures into the computer and scanned for her favorites. *Where do I start?* At the beginning, and the beginning in this case was language school in Romania. The only two volunteers fresh out of college, Carrie and Michelle had formed a friendship that grew even stronger when they returned home two years later. When they left Romania, Michelle didn't expect to move to Denver on the strength of Carrie's recommendation.

After Joe displayed the album in his store, Michelle planned to give it to Carrie as a present, a testimony to a special friendship and a fairy-tale romance. The file of "must include" pictures quickly grew. She was glad she had caught Steve and Carrie on camera several times while they were still in Romania.

From there she selected shots of the bridal shower, rehearsal dinner, the ceremony, and reception. Michelle slowed down as she looked at each picture, her mind deceiving her by superimposing Joe's face over Steve's in each shot. *Focus*, Michelle scolded herself. *Stop fantasizing*.

She stumbled on a snapshot she had forgotten. A light snow fell all day on the day of the wedding. Steve and Carrie left the church, with him tucking Carrie protectively under his arm to shield her. Compassion and commitment and love were stamped on his face as clearly as a redhead's freckles.

Tears sprang to Michelle's eyes. She wanted that for herself, for Joe, but for some reason he didn't seem to think he was worthy. Maybe she imagined that more existed between them than was truly there. They needed time and distance to sort things out.

eleven

I can't believe I'm doing this, in spite of the promises I made myself to create some distance from Joe. Less than two weeks had passed since Joe had left Denver. Michelle checked her odometer. The exit leading to Ulysses should be coming up in a mile.

"Blink, and you'll miss it," Joe had explained when he invited her to come to Ulysses for the annual Odyssey Days. He paused a second before he added, "Once you're off the highway, you'd have to blink twice to miss Ulysses." She could still hear his chuckle down the line.

A few silos rose above the prairie, but she saw no other signs of settlement except for cultivated fields as far as the eye could see. For the first time Michelle realized how isolated Ulysses was and marveled at how Joe had grown a successful business.

South of the highway, one building's outline changed as she neared it. Michelle squinted, not believing what her eyes saw. A castle rose like a sentinel above the prairie, as out of place as a snowstorm in July. She'd have to ask Joe about it.

At the exit, a small sign announced ULYSSES 3 MILES. Michelle turned onto the narrow road. The distant cluster of buildings grew larger. She was meeting Joe at his store. He promised to stay late until she arrived after work on Friday night. "Just park anywhere along Main Street," he advised. "Then look for my store, the Trojan Horse."

The posted speed limit dropped to forty before the town began and then twenty-five as she rounded a bend in the road, and she saw the city limit sign. A truck roared past, country music blasting from the stereo. Trucks outnumbered cars three to one at the hamburger stand. Kids ran up and down the sidewalks. *Friday night in a small town.*

Over Main Street, a banner hung suspended between two tall columns announcing 35TH ANNUAL ODYSSEY DAYS, JULY 21–22. Lamps fashioned to look like torches sat atop ivy-entwined light poles.

She slowed down and spotted a wooden horse painted on a shop window. Like the fabled horse, its side pivoted open to reveal beautiful treasures inside. A small sign announced PARKING AVAILABLE IN BACK. She slipped her car in front.

Joe hustled out the door and enfolded Michelle in a bear hug. "You made it."

He looked so happy, sunshine itself radiating from his eyes, a face as carefree as if life had not yet made him wary of disappointment. He had shed ten years in two weeks. "Welcome to Ulysses." He relaxed his hold. "Come inside."

Michelle hadn't quite known what to expect, perhaps something like an art museum, but nothing prepared her for what greeted her eyes when she entered the store. The late-day sun filtered through the window, casting a golden glow over white plaster walls. Paintings hung on the walls, and other pieces—wood carvings, pottery, steel sculptures— sat displayed atop Grecian columns of different heights. The atmosphere most resembled an ancient grotto. Like at the gates to the Renaissance Festival, she felt like she had entered another world.

"This is fantastic. And it looks like you've found buyers for several things already," she added, noting the SOLD signs on some of the paintings.

"Yeah, I've done pretty well this week. C'mon. There's more."

The back room created an entirely different world—a play haven for children, with a pottery wheel, painting easel, building blocks, and tables ranging in size from preschool to adult. A model car Viktor had assembled was on display, as well as artwork by people of various ages. Shelves held art magazines, how-to books, and coffee table tomes with full-color photographs.

"We offer different art classes during the year. Right now we're doing pottery—always a favorite."

"Children, too?"

"Of course." He grinned at her. "Wait 'til you see it tomorrow. Sometimes it feels like all one thousand residents of Ulysses plus most of their friends throughout the county traipse through here on weekends. The rest of the week I keep busy handling sales online."

"The store is open tomorrow?"

"Busiest day of the week."

What about our day together?

"Don't worry. I'll be here in the morning, but we'll close shop for Odyssey Days in the afternoon."

Michelle hoped the relief didn't show too clearly on her face.

Joe checked his watch. "Speaking of my mother, she's expecting us for supper. She'll never forgive me if I'm late for her pot roast." He walked Michelle out to her car, holding her hand as if it was the most natural thing in the world. Goose bumps of pleasure pimpled Michelle's skin from her shoulder to her wrist.

Joe sketched a map to his mother's house.

"Why don't I just follow you?" Michelle asked, staring at the crossing lines and directions like "red barn—two more miles."

"In case we get separated. Besides, don't worry. You can't

miss it. My mother added her own unique twist to the old family homestead." He spread his hands as if words failed him. "You'll see."

Michelle wondered briefly what that meant, but Joe's mother must be as nice as he was. They headed south and west out of town, parallel to the highway, driving up a slight incline. Acres of green corn and wheat waved in the dusk sky, with occasional fields with cows grazing on tall grass. She saw nothing out of the ordinary until they crested the hill.

It can't be. But it is. Michelle gulped in surprise. Straight ahead of them stood the castle she had seen from the interstate, now a black silhouette against a fiery sky. Guard towers rose from three corners of a flat roof, and a tall circular turret rose into the sky at the entrance. A proliferation of flowers like an English garden surrounded the walls. It looked more like a baronial estate than a farmhouse in Colorado.

Sir Cameron. Now it makes sense. And no wonder his mother needs help. If Joe's mother lives like this, what is the rest of his family like? And how big is his family? Two cars and three trucks, including Joe's, were already parked in the yard.

Joe barely made it to her door before two slight figures raced around the edge of the house and hid behind his back, weighing down his arms like two millstones.

"Let me go. You'll have your chance. I want to help Michelle out of the car."

"That's not necessary." She unfolded herself from the low-lying seat with a minimum of fuss.

"Be nice now, girls," Joe whispered to the figures still hidden behind his back.

"We will, we promise." Different-sized versions of the same red-haired, freckled-faced girl pressed in front of Joe, thrusting a nosegay of flowers at Michelle.

"These are for you," the taller girl said.

"We picked them all by ourselves," the younger girl added proudly.

Michelle fussed over the wilting flowers, touched by the gesture.

"An' Grannie let us pick a rose for you to wear in your hair." The littlest girl handed Michelle an open rose with dark red petals as soft as velvet. "We chose red 'cause it's the color of love." She drawled out the word.

"That's enough now, girls." Joe's cheeks turned as red as the rose. Michelle pretended not to notice and tucked the rose behind her ear.

"May I present my nieces? Pepper"—he indicated the taller girl—"and Poppy." He pointed to a girl who couldn't be older than three.

Pepper? Poppy?

"Nicknames," Joe confirmed in answer to her unspoken question. "We're big into nicknames around here."

Like Joe. With hair as fiery as cayenne pepper and as brilliant as the poppy flower, Michelle could guess how the girls had come by their nicknames.

"Our real names are Teresa and Christina. But only Grannie ever calls us that," Pepper said.

"Cameron?" a cultured voice called. The chatelaine of the castle waited, ready to receive her guest. With her stood a couple, the man with a strong family resemblance to Joe and a woman with hair as red as the girls'.

"Grannie, she's here," Pepper announced.

Michelle hadn't known what to expect from the woman who called the castle home. Aside from her formal attire, compared to everyone else's casual jeans, she looked ordinary. "Aren't you going to introduce us, son?" The lady strolled over the lawn as if it were red carpet. "You must be Michelle." She extended a manicured hand in greeting. "Welcome to my home, my dear." Her smile was as warm and welcoming as Joe's, and Michelle felt at ease.

❧

"Good night." Joe waved good-bye to his brother's family as they drove away in their truck. He breathed a sigh of relief. *Phew, that went better than I expected.*

"They're nice," Michelle said. "That's something that gets lost in the city, a sense of roots. Your brother's the town doctor, right?"

"And my father was, too, until he died." Joe cleared his throat. "And my grandfather before that. I'm the odd one out, opting to tilt after windmills instead."

"I don't know that I'd call running a business tilting after windmills."

Bless you for that. "So you don't find it too strange?"

"I don't know about that." Michelle chuckled. "I've never been entertained in a castle before."

"Yes, well, it was my father's wedding present to my mother. So she wouldn't miss England too much."

"How charming." Hand in hand, they walked across the lawn—the grass had grown a little high, he needed to mow it soon—surrounding his mother's home. Michelle's hair fell over her shoulders, a slight wind lifting the ends. She looked like she belonged, a princess at ease on a baronial estate.

"So your mother is from England?" Michelle followed her own train of thought.

"My grandmother was. Mother spent most of her summers there when she was growing up."

"Oh," was Michelle's only comment.

Oh, as in, isn't that interesting? Oh, as in, no wonder she's so strange? Forget about Mother. Joe led Michelle to a canopied double swing inside the rose arbor. "Shh. Relax. Listen." Joe nudged the ground with his toe and rocked the seat.

Fireflies flickered in the velvet night sky. Moisture from an earlier shower gathered the scent of roses, filling Joe's nostrils with their sweet fragrance. The hoot of an owl, the gentle neighing of horses, cows bawling—the noise of a country evening throbbed through the air.

Late evening twilight darkened to deepest night, lit by a thousand stars. They sat long minutes without speaking. The peace of the evening permeated Joe's body, conquering all of the day's accumulated tension. Crickets sang in rhythm with the swing, the sound soothing enough to lull an insomniac to sleep. *Let all mortal flesh keep silence.* Out here man was silent, and all nature sang the praise of their Creator. "Do you hear it, Michelle? Do you hear the song of the plains?" Joe held his breath. Her answer mattered—a lot.

"Yes." She snuggled closer to his chest. "But only because I'm here with you."

Joe looked down, gazing at her upturned face, features transformed into precious alabaster by the moonlight. He saw a reflection of the desires of his own heart.

At last Sir Cameron claimed his kiss from Lady Michelle.

twelve

How long they kissed, arms entwined about each other, Michelle couldn't guess. She only knew that her pulse roared in her ears loud enough to drown out the crickets, and the light in Joe's eyes outshone the constellations of the sky. She felt his chin with her hand, fingers touching the slight imperfection where he had nicked himself shaving, the bristles reappearing. This was her Joe, bumps, bristles, and all.

He loosened his embrace and kissed her chastely on the forehead, as a knight should. His breath came out ragged. "I've dreamed of doing that for a long time."

"Me, too. It was"—Michelle groped for a word—"nice." *Fool. You say "nice" about a person's appearance or personality.* Not about a kiss that she felt down to her toes, that sealed the sense of rightness of loving Joe.

"And now I'd better see you inside." Joe stopped the swing. "Before my mother catches me kissing you again."

In the dark, Michelle could sense more than see his grin. Walking over the graveled pathway to the castle gate, she danced down a lane sprinkled with fairy dust. If she pinched herself, would she wake up from the dream? More importantly, could her feelings for Joe stand up to the light of day and the pressures of the real world?

She shook the questions away. She refused to let practical questions ruin the magic of the evening. *But that's what you came to Ulysses for—to see if there is more to your love for Joe than some fairy-tale romance.* Her conscience refused to quit.

In the courtyard, Joe kissed her once more, briefly, on the

lips. They stood holding hands. "Are you ready to come in?" Mrs. Knight stood silhouetted against light glowing from inside the castle.

"I'm just leaving, Mother." Bending forward, he whispered in Michelle's ear. "Go with God." He let go of her hands and climbed in his truck.

Michelle wrenched her gaze from the road where the taillights disappeared. She joined her hostess inside the fortress—as if stone and mortar could protect her from the emotions thundering through her body.

"Thanks for dinner, Mrs. Knight. It was delicious."

"Call me Nel." The words were more command than invitation. "You must be tired after your trip from Denver. I'll show you to your room." Grabbing Michelle's overnight bag in one hand, she headed for the staircase at the opposite end of the entrance hall.

Large tapestries hung on the walls, and Michelle stopped long enough to study them. "That must be your family's coat of arms." She identified a unicorn and a bear facing off against each other, intertwined by cords of heavy rope.

"Yes. My ancestors on my mother's side came to England with William the Conqueror." A definite note of pride vibrated through Mrs. Knight's voice.

What was it like to know centuries of your family's history? As far as Michelle knew, her ancestry was a typical American melting pot, British by name, Scandinavian by complexion, with a dash of eastern European mixed in. Beyond American shores, she didn't know her history at all.

Opposite the tapestry with the coat of arms hung a beautifully embroidered gigantic letter *I*. Michelle approached it. Vines trailed from the *I*, forming a border around the verse quoted on the hanging, appearing much like a monk's illumination of a page of the Bible.

The letter *I* began a quote from the Bible. She read the words aloud. "It is better to trust in the Lord than to put confidence in man. It is better to trust in the Lord than to put confidence in princes. Psalm 118:8–9."

"I see you've discovered our family motto." Mrs. Knight didn't give the picture a second glance.

"Did you make it yourself?" Michelle asked, admiring the intricate needlework utilized in the pattern, although a patina of age gave sheen to the material.

"Me? Oh no. It was done by my great-grandmother when she waited for news of her husband and son during the Great War. A reminder that only God is our true refuge. A lesson that my knight-errant son still needs to learn."

"I've noticed." Memories of Joe challenging Sir Roland flooded her mind. "He seems to think it's his sworn duty to protect me from all harm."

"I know." They climbed wide stone steps, covered by a thin carpet to help ward off the chill. "I talked about the chivalrous ideal a lot when the boys were small. Better than the violence on the nightly news."

"It's rather sweet," Michelle said in defense of Joe. "But—"

"But my younger son carries things a bit too far. Confronting bullies more than twice his size in grade school. Inviting two girls to the prom because he was afraid neither one would be asked."

Michelle smiled at the image of a young Joe, handsome in a tuxedo à la James Bond, fighting off bad guys with one hand while two lovely girls clung to his other arm.

Further discussion ended when they arrived at the guest room, named the Rosebriar. Michelle stepped over the threshold into a fantasy of pink. Someone had fluffed the king-sized bed high enough to make her wonder if she were being tested like the princess and the pea. A canopy fluttered in the breeze from the open window.

"I hope you like it." Mrs. Knight—*Nel*—hung Michelle's few clothes in the closet. "With two boys demanding variations of knights on chargers, I indulged myself in this room. Your privy is through this door."

Michelle peeked in after her hostess and was relieved to see the usual modern conveniences.

"Find it a bit much, do you?" Mrs. Knight's pink-silvered lips curled in a smile. "Most people do."

"It's charming, Mrs.—I mean, Nel."

Nel patted Michelle on the arm. "I'm in the opposite tower, if you need anything." With a quiet rustle of silk, she left Michelle alone in her room.

Michelle sponged her face, enjoying the cool water against her hot skin. She slipped on a white organza nightgown, relishing the feel of the smooth fabric, and perused the other items on the stand. She peeked into a handheld mirror—too small for anything besides fixing her hair. She was glad for the full-length mirror in the washroom. An immaculate silver brush and comb set with a rose etched into their handles shone, inviting use.

She tested the weight of the brush in her hand and slowly lifted it to her head. She brushed her hair with long, firm strokes in rhythm with the song of the crickets outside the window.

Lady Michelle brushes her hair to a pale gold. She wants to please her knight when he returns. She pinches her cheeks for a bit of color.

Ouch. The painful pinch brought Michelle back to reality. She shook her head. Enough of playacting for the night. No wonder Joe had trouble separating reality from make-believe, growing up in a house like this one. It seduced the susceptible into a simpler time. What did he need more?

Someone with her feet planted firmly on the ground—or someone to dream with?

Oh Joe. Warm memories of their kiss flooded over her, infusing her with fresh confidence. *We're right for each other. I know it.*

ঽ

Joe awakened as the midsummer sunrise streamed into his room. By his bedside Gawain stretched his long body forward and back and stuck a cold nose against Joe's cheek.

"Ready for a morning run, huh?" Gawain would settle down if Joe turned over, but he felt as eager as the dog for the day to begin. He shrugged into a faded T-shirt and running shorts and headed out the door, the Lab at his heels.

No need today for headphones to drown out the she-loves-me-she-loves-me-not litany of the past week. Instead his feet pounded in time with his heart, singing—no, shouting—a love song to the skies. Michelle's kiss had branded his soul. He couldn't wait to show her around Ulysses. He hoped she loved it as much as he did. She had accepted his eccentric mother without as much as blinking her eyes. Appreciating his hometown should come easily after that.

The day had already started to warm up when he drove to his mother's home a short time later. Gawain sat beside him in the truck, as proud as the griffins standing guard at the entrance to the castle.

"Stay." He jumped out of the cab. Gawain ignored his command and followed him through the front doors.

Joe found his mother and Michelle in the kitchen, a long narrow room. They huddled together at one corner of the table, Michelle wrist-deep in flour. One tray of triangular-shaped pieces of dough rested beside her, and his mother was pulling a second one out of the oven. He watched the two women sharing a laugh. *Better and better.*

"Joe." Michelle beamed with such obvious joy that he took a step in her direction, drawn by a magnet beyond his control.

"Your mother is showing me how to make real scones. Here, try one." She lifted the rich, buttery bread to his mouth, so close that when he took a bite, his mouth brushed her fingers. The intimacy of the touch sent a shiver to his toes. Michelle jerked her hand away as if burned.

"Mmm, good."

Gawain growled and planted himself at Joe's feet, forcing space between them. Joe's chest tightened. He had never seen Michelle around animals. Did she even like them?

He didn't need to worry. Michelle reached out to pet him and then stared at her flour-covered hands. Instead she bent over and went nose-to-nose with the dog. "You're a sweet boy—yes, you are." The Lab's tail wagged, indicating he was her slave for life. *Just like me.* "He's beautiful. What's his name?"

"Gawain." Joe looked sheepish when he mentioned the unlikely name. "King Arthur's nephew. He was one of the Knights of the Round Table."

"Of course." Michelle laughed. "Pleased to make your acquaintance, Sir Gawain." She rubbed noses with the dog one more time and straightened up. "Someday I'll have a place where I can have a dog again."

How well Joe remembered the struggle in the city to find a place to rent for someone with a dog, especially a big dog like a Labrador. Sonia had grudgingly kept him a few times when Joe went out of town. *Love me, love my dog.* And Michelle liked dogs.

After a very American meal of bacon and eggs and coffee, the only English touches being the fresh-baked scones and tea for his mother, Joe and Michelle headed to town. He pulled up in front of his store, which waited as always for someone to flip the switch and bring it to life. His palms slipped on the wheel. Would Michelle like his work enough to want to be a part of it? This morning he might find part of the answer.

Up and down Main Street people were raising shades and opening doors. His first customers should arrive within fifteen minutes. Michelle would love the mixture of clientele that came through the store on a festival weekend like Odyssey Days. He just knew it.

&

"Miss?" A white-haired waif tugged at Michelle's arm. "Did I do this right?"

Michelle turned from the twins she was helping to the girl holding a misshapen lump. Beyond a body and a head, she couldn't decipher what kind of animal it was supposed to be. "I like it. Tell me about it."

Joe peeked over her shoulder. "That's an interesting spider you have there."

"It's not a spider." The child held it up for closer inspection. "It's a cat."

"That's funny." Joe frowned. "I could have sworn I saw eight legs, ready to crawl up your arm." He ran his fingers across the table like a bug, and she giggled.

Michelle enjoyed watching Joe with the children. He had a knack for communicating with little ones. *He'll be a good father.* She smiled at the thought.

In any case, the children's workshops worked well for Joe. One or two small bodies crammed onto every seat in the back room of Joe's shop. He said the Saturday morning classes brought in a lot of money. Judging from the number of children at this Creating with Clay session, he hadn't exaggerated.

Michelle labeled all the works in progress and set them on the shelf. A fire engine siren blared in the distance, and the room emptied.

Joe tugged her arm. "C'mon. The parade's starting. We can watch from the front."

She pushed chairs under the table, rushing to leave.

"We'll miss the grand marshal. It's the high school principal this year."

Michelle hung back, staring about the now-empty store. "But what about the shop?"

"It's closed this afternoon for the festival." Joe pulled her outside, where the hot summer air pinned her blouse to her back like a dry cleaner's bag even as it seared her throat. They could see the lead motorcycle cops, lights flashing, horns beeping. She couldn't believe she saw an actual Dalmatian riding next to the ladder on the fire engine, surveying the scene as if he were the king.

"I wonder how they'll handle this year's theme—Quest for Success," Joe said. "Ah, there's the bank float."

Letters reading BANK WITH US—WE'LL GUIDE YOUR QUEST adorned the sides of the flatbed. Two seekers in Grecian costumes worked their way through a maze to a treasure of homes, cars, and cash.

Joe studied the float. "So that's why they needed the purple paint."

"Do you help plan any of the floats?" After all, he was in essence the resident art expert.

"Me? No. I tried it once. It's too much work for me by myself. But I always donate some of the supplies. Tit for tat. It brings in business."

Children danced by in semiragged rows. Michelle spotted a head of red hair and waved and then returned to fanning her face with a newspaper. "That was Pepper, right?"

Joe grinned, waving wildly.

Men in clown suits rode by on oversized tricycles, tossing candy to the crowd. Soon the strains of horns and drums announced the arrival of the high school band. Girls whirled by in Grecian robes, tossing column-like batons in the air. Togas in blue and gold—the school colors, Michelle assumed—covered white uniforms. The drum major marched by, a girl in a golden helmet instead of the more traditional plumed hat. She lifted her arms to initiate a drum roll, and the gold button on her tunic slipped down her shoulder.

Michelle sponged away the sweat from her forehead. Heat clamped its hand on her throat, making it difficult for her to breathe. *If it gets any hotter, I'm going to faint.* Black dots floated behind her eyelids as she crumpled to the ground.

thirteen

Someone pressed a cool cloth against Michelle's forehead, and large fingers checked her pulse.

"Is she gonna be okay?" a small voice piped somewhere behind her head.

"I'm fine, really." Michelle's words came out somewhere between a whimper and a groan. When she tried to sit up, she couldn't lift her head.

"She's coming around," a deep voice said. "Give her room. She needs air." Feet shuffled as people moved away.

This time Michelle succeeded in opening her eyes. Someone had moved her inside Joe's store. Two men knelt beside her, resembling one another enough so that for a moment she thought she was seeing double—Joe and his brother Brian. Her head rested on Joe's lap. His sister-in-law Judy clasped her legs. Poppy held the washcloth to her head. With the Knights, family medicine took on a new meaning. Perhaps they played games of Operation with pretend patients. A giggle burbled from her throat.

"Here. Drink this." Joe's strong arms lifted her to a sitting position, cradling her head against his rock-solid chest. She sipped the water and the light-headedness that had sent her plunging to the ground receded.

"I put on sunblock this morning, I don't know what happened." She stood on her own, a chair providing sturdy support.

Nel appeared in the doorway, flourishing a wide-brimmed straw hat that would fit in at Wimbledon. "Wear this," she instructed Michelle in her best "mom" voice. "It will keep the sun off your face." Given the imperious note in Nel's voice, Michelle felt compelled to don it.

Joe smiled at Michelle, whether from relief or in appreciation of her appearance, she couldn't tell. "I'll be back in a minute." He left the room.

Police sirens sounded, and Poppy ran to the window. Judy turned to Michelle. "Glad you're feeling better. I have to find Pepper." She took her daughter outside.

Brian hung around a minute longer. "I don't think it's serious. Keep drinking water. The hat's a good idea, Mother." He paused, as if uncertain whether he was the doctor or the concerned brother at this point. "You know where to find me."

Michelle wished everyone would depart and leave her alone. Passing out was embarrassing enough without all this fuss.

"Are you sure you want to stay? I could take you home." Nel patted Michelle's hand, and she thought about accepting.

"Michelle?" Joe reappeared, holding a glass jar filled with ice cubes and water. "Are you ready to rejoin the festivities?"

Nel opened her mouth but waited for Michelle's response.

What should she do? A day in the quiet coolness of the castle gardens held great appeal, like a chance to go to Disney World instead of the county fair. But she had come to Ulysses to spend the day with Joe. She smiled at him. "Yeah. I'm fine."

"You two go on. I'll lock up here." Nel waved them out the door. "Should I expect you for dinner?"

"I thought about heading over to the steak place." Joe bounced on his heels like a boy waiting for his turn at bat, displaying the same boyish quality that alternately charmed and infuriated Michelle.

More time with Joe. "That sounds good." She placed her

hand in Joe's, and when he grinned at her, the world spun to the right position. She didn't want for anything more than Joe by her side.

❧

"We missed the end of the parade." A wistful note crept into Joe's voice. He hoped Michelle didn't think he blamed her.

"I'm glad I got to see Pepper dance. She's so cute. What's next?"

"If we hurry, we can still make it for the presentation of Queen Penelope's court."

"Who was Penelope anyway?" Michelle plopped his mother's hat on her head, and it transformed her into an English lady. "Or Ulysses for that matter? I've forgotten a lot of my mythology since high school."

"Ulysses, or Odysseus if you use his Greek name, went off to fight the Trojan War—Homer immortalized the story in *The Odyssey.* Penelope was his wife. She waited for Ulysses to return for twenty years. Convinced he was dead, suitors vied for her hand. She promised to choose between them as soon as she finished her weaving—only every night she tore apart what she had sewn during the day."

Michelle giggled. They approached the park in the center of town. A raised platform sat along one side. Dozens of booths crowded the small area with a large tent standing in the middle, perhaps the center for food and drink.

Joe made his way through the crowd, finding Brian and his family by the platform. Pepper and Poppy stared at the candidates in open admiration.

"I hope I'm Queen Penelope someday." Pepper gazed with adoring eyes as a floral garland was placed on the head of a fair-headed farm girl with a winsome smile.

"That would be nice," her mother agreed. "Or you might win the state spelling bee—"

"Or the state science fair," her father added.

"Or even your softball tournament," Joe said.

"Whatever you do, we'll always be proud of you," Judy concluded.

Joe's attention drifted during the presentation speeches, rendered unintelligible by the excessive amplification. He noticed people casting quick, curious glances at Michelle, and pride surged through him at the beautiful woman at his side. How lucky he was.

Before long, curiosity overcame shyness. Hugh Classen, the high school art teacher, ambled over, his two young boys at his heels. "Hey, Joe, want to introduce us?"

Joe made introductions and admired the way Michelle responded to his friend. She grasped Hugh's hand firmly, not the wilted-cabbage handshake some women affected. A warm smile accompanied a look straight in the eye. "Pleased to meet you, Mr. Classen."

"Hugh, please."

"Pleased to meet you, Hugh. And who are these handsome young men?"

Even after the tenth such introduction, Michelle continued to exude genuine interest in each person. They meandered around the park, stopping at every stall. Joe tried his hand at a few of the show-off booths. That was what he called the places that challenged guys to shoot a duck or toss a ring over a bottle and win a prize for the lady. He failed, more or less on purpose, until they reached the darts booth. "Here's another one."

She groaned. She looked right at home, one hand clutching a plastic bag full of freebies and the other lifting the remains of a wand of purple cotton candy to her mouth. "You don't have to throw any more money away on carnies for me." She wiped a smidgen of purple dye from the edge of her mouth.

Joe resisted the urge to kiss it away. "I'll have you know I'm supporting the"—he squinted at a small sign at the back of the booth—"the local Ducks Unlimited. My favorite charity. Three chances, please." He handed a dollar bill to the carny.

The object of the game was to puncture balloons of various sizes with darts. The smaller the balloon, the bigger the prize.

Joe took aim.

Pop. "Yellow for hope."

Pop. "And green for renewal."

Pop. "And finally, red for love."

He had shattered three of the smallest balloons. "I'll take the large black dog, please." He turned to Michelle with the Gawain look-alike. "You said you wanted a dog. Even the fussiest landlord can't object to this fellow."

She hugged the dog so tightly that he would have stopped breathing if he were alive. "It's great. Wherever did you learn to throw darts like that?"

"It was as easy as taking candy from a baby." They moved away from the booth, Michelle's face dwarfed by the gigantic toy. "Don't you know that throwing darts is an English obsession?"

"And your mother—"

"My mother challenges me every chance she gets." He tossed a pebble into the air. "I actually beat her every now and then."

When Michelle stubbed her toe on a power cable she couldn't see because of the stuffed animal, Joe insisted that he carry it. His free hand reached for Michelle's. "Too bad that dog doesn't have a recorder inside. He could whisper sweet nothings in your ear when we're apart."

"What would he say?"

"That you make me feel all three, you know—hope, renewal, love."

Michelle turned away shyly, her cheeks turning a delicate pink.

"At the least he can be your guardian angel dog."

Michelle giggled, some of the embarrassment receding.

A moment later they ran into Brian's family. Poppy's eyes grew as big as pennies at the sight of the stuffed animal. "Where did you get that?"

"Playing darts." Joe imitated the throw.

"He's beautiful." Before Joe could warn Michelle about Poppy's propensity to beg, the girl said, "I wish I had one like him."

Michelle laughed and glanced at Joe. "Then he's yours."

"Really?"

"Really." Michelle took the animal out of Joe's arms and set it on the ground next to Poppy. "He's a very special dog. Joe gave him to me to watch over me, and now I'll tell him to watch over you."

"Thanks." Poppy threw her arms around Michelle. The dog was taller than the child, and Brian had to take it. "We'll take this out to the car. See you later, Joe, Michelle."

Joe watched the departing toy with regret. "I got that for you. But that was sweet of you."

"Oh Joe. I don't need a stuffed dog. . .and I'll always remember what you said."

As if in slow motion Joe's fingers caressed her face. He leaned close, wanting to seal the moment with a kiss, to capture the new closeness between them.

"There you are." His mother swung around the corner, scattering the two lovers like pigeons at the approach of a car. "I was hoping Michelle would judge the pie contest for me."

જ

Michelle couldn't decide whether Nel's interruption relieved or disappointed her more. What would Nel think of her face, heated as it was? She glanced at Joe. Warmth shone from his eyes, comforting her with a sense of love and security. His mouth twisted as if disappointed at the unexpected interruption.

Nel swept on. "This is the first time they asked me to judge the contest, but two of my best friends have entered. I can't possibly judge between them. Please, do help me out." Her regal smile was more command than invitation.

"Good idea, Mother." Joe whispered in Michelle's ear, "Please say yes. It's too much for Mum." Turning back to his mother, he said, "Michelle will find something kind to say about every entry, even if it tastes like it was made with apples from last year's crop cooked between cardboard crusts."

Heartened by Joe's affirmation, Michelle let Nel lead her in the direction of the contest arena. No sweet smells indicated the trail. Like Hansel's bread crumbs, they had been devoured, not by birds, but by the mixture of diesel fumes, animal odors, and the press of humanity common to every fair.

Half a dozen anxious women hovered around a table, ranging from a young mother with a baby in her arms to a senior citizen too experienced to let her nervousness show. A middle-aged woman as thin and angular as a tree in November marched in their direction.

"Nel. Now that you're here, we can get started." She spoke with the confidence of someone who expected to win.

"To tell the truth, Esther, I've abdicated. This lovely young woman with me is Michelle Morris. She helped me bake this morning, and from what I observed, she's well qualified to judge." She graced Esther with the same regal smile and maneuvered Michelle into a corner where she could whisper instructions. "Here are the tally sheets. Appearance is always a good place to award extra points even if the pie tastes terrible."

Nel's nose wrinkled ever so slightly. "Esther has won for

the last three years, but young Molly is hoping she'll win the contest and use it as a springboard to start her own bakery. In case you're wondering, the pies are unmarked, so cut a small piece of each. You don't have to eat more than a bite or two." Speaking loudly enough so the crowd could hear, she added, "Thanks to all of you for participating. And good luck."

Michelle sidled up to the table and tried to look like she knew what she was doing. A wide assortment of pies greeted her—meringue, lattice-top, graham cracker crust, crumb topping. How could she compare them? The meringue was high and fluffy, perfectly sealed to the edge. She bent down to check the graham cracker crust through the glass pie pan—perfect. The strips of the lattice top were even, glistening with sprinkled sugar. In fact, the only thing she could fault in appearance of any of the candidates was a small overly brown section of the two-crust pie. So far, so good. She made notes on the clipboard Nel had handed her.

Silence reigned over their corner of the festivities. Grasping the knife, Michelle cut a tiny wedge of what appeared to be apple pie. The piece slid easily out of the pan, a smidgen of flaky crust dropping to the side. The pastry was excellent, but nutmeg and allspice overwhelmed the flavor of the filling. Not a winner. She set down her fork and wiped her mouth.

No one moved as Michelle wrote on the score sheet, "Wonderful crust—perhaps rethink the spices."

The other pies were perfect examples of their kinds— fluffy meringue that melted in her mouth over a decadent chocolate filling, a lattice pie chock-full of blueberries with just the right amount of sugar. She left the graham cracker crust to last because it resembled nothing so much as a no-bake cheesecake, yellow custard in appearance that could taste like lemon or banana or even vanilla.

The last pie was in fact a flan-like banana custard, chunks

of fruit in the mix, rich caramel on the bottom, dots of whipped cream across the surface, and a trace of cinnamon in the crust. Michelle knew she had found the winner.

She made appropriate comments on the tally sheets. "I love blueberries," and "Just the right spices for the crumb topping." Ribbons in hand, she looked at Nel, wondering how to proceed.

"Speech. Speech." Joe grinned at her from the sidelines.

She changed her look of concentration to the most welcoming smile she could muster. "First of all, let me say all your pies are delicious. I couldn't bake pies like these if my life depended on it."

The tension level increased although no one said anything.

"Because the pie was perfectly done, third place goes to"—Michelle turned over the name card—"Mary Robbins, for her lemon meringue pie."

A bubbly, round lady who looked like she spent a lot of time in the kitchen beamed her happiness as she accepted the ribbon.

"Because it was as beautiful as it was delicious, second place goes to"—a quick glance at the card—"Laura Simmons, for her blueberry pie."

An elderly lady slipped forward, hands fluttering. "Oh my, I never expected."

Michelle wondered which participant had baked the award-winning pie, but resisted the urge to peek at the name card she held in her hand. "One of the pies stood above the rest—exotic, unique in its flavor. First place goes to"—now she checked—"Molly Perkins, for her banana flan pie."

Even as the delighted young woman stepped forward to receive the award, Esther flew at Nel.

"How could you pawn this woman off on us as an expert? She obviously doesn't know what she's talking about."

fourteen

Nel silenced Esther with a look, a regal glare that would silence all but the most obnoxious reporters at a press conference. "Congratulations to the winners. And a special thanks to Michelle Morris for her assistance in judging." She clapped her hands together once, and a smattering of applause broke out. She spoke a word or two to each winner before she swept Michelle away from the furious Esther.

Nel walked at a deliberate pace in the direction of the Midway with Joe trailing behind, but a small laughing hiccup drew attention to the merriment in her eyes. "That was priceless." The wide grin that captured her face testified to her effort to restrain laughter. "Someone finally was able to let Esther know how awful her apple pie is."

"She made that apple pie? I didn't say anything about it."

"You didn't have to, child. The fact that she didn't win said it all. Molly's shop is off to a good start, and two of my friends were runners-up. How nice."

"Esther was so full of herself, I was rather pleased when she didn't win," Michelle admitted. "Not that I did it on purpose. I didn't know—"

"Of course not," Joe chortled. "I wouldn't have missed it for the world."

All thousand residents of Ulysses probably connected in a myriad of ways. Best friends, bitter enemies, new rivals, third and fourth cousins. The Chicago neighborhood where she grew up had some of the same qualities, but it felt stronger here. Today she was the outsider looking in and wished she could share in Nel and Joe's glee.

ِ❧

"After all that pie, do you still have room for supper?" Joe asked.

"Maybe something light. Does Ulysses have any salad bars?"

Joe's stomach tightened in protest. Watching Michelle sample half a dozen mouth-watering pies had accelerated his appetite, not dampened it. "The steak place I mentioned earlier has a salad bar." Hand in hand, they headed for the parking lot. Half the people they met greeted Michelle warmly, news of her pie-judging exploits already spreading through the crowd.

Michelle responded in kind, remembering everyone's names, a smile springing to her face whenever someone stopped to say hello. Joe's stomach growled low, complaining about the delay in mealtime.

Hugh Classen approached, his shirt the worse for wear with a few ketchup stains. "What do you think of Odyssey Days?"

"It's been great. And have you boys had fun?" She winked at them, and in return they displayed their temporary tattoos proudly.

She did it again. Joe wondered how many more people would stop them on the way out. He began to feel like he had crashed his own party. His grip on her arm tightened, and Michelle slid a sideways glance in his direction.

"Is there a more direct way out of here?" She must have sensed his feelings.

"Not really." He shrugged.

"I guess I don't want the day to end. I've had such fun." But the next time someone called a greeting, she waved and continued walking at a brisk pace. Soon they reached the car.

"Do you want to freshen up first?" Joe felt the layers of sweaty grime and a five o'clock shadow on his own face. He had something important to say to Michelle tonight, and he knew he didn't look his best.

"I can't." Michelle giggled. "The only other clothing I brought is my dress for tomorrow." She brushed a stray pie crumb from her blouse and frowned. "The steak place isn't fancy, is it?" She rubbed at a stain on her blouse.

Concern over his own appearance melted away. "You're perfect." He pulled her in close and kissed her briefly to let her know she was beautiful and desirable.

She pillowed her head on his shoulder and played with the top button of his shirt. "Thanks."

A few people threw curious glances in their direction, but Joe ignored them, rejoicing in the feeling of Michelle in his arms. After a few moments Michelle separated from him and straightened her back, a confident grin in place. He wished he could help keep it there all the time. "Shall we go then?"

About a quarter of an hour later they stood in line at the restaurant, waiting to place their orders. Signed autographs from rodeo stars and country singers lined the walls, with the obligatory rack of elk antlers at the door.

"What fun," Michelle said. "I haven't been in a place like this for years. My goodness, there's a picture of Bill Pickett."

"You know about Pickett?" That surprised Joe.

"Of course. He was my brother's hero when he was a kid. He dreamed of being a rodeo rider until he grew up and went to dental school instead." Internal mirth curved her lips.

"Yeah, maybe he'll strike up a business replacing teeth knocked out in the ring." They laughed lightly.

They had arrived at the cashier. Joe ordered a sixteen-ounce T-bone and wondered if it would be enough to satisfy his hunger. Michelle stuck with the salad bar. They both went to the large table in the middle of the room. Joe took a little of the green stuff but also added a generous helping of potato salad and carrot-raisin salad and two of the perfectly browned yeast rolls with a generous slather of butter. Michelle chose a high pile of lettuce leaves, tomatoes, and bean sprouts, topped with a light dressing and a couple of bread sticks, then added a grilled chicken breast from the buffet. No wonder she stayed so slender.

Joe led them to a secluded corner of the restaurant, away from the salad-bar traffic, not that they had any privacy. Crowds from the fair filled every table, and Joe almost had to shout to make himself heard.

During dinner, several well-wishers and curiosity seekers stopped by the table. Under the strain of constant interruptions, Michelle's friendliness eroded a little. They sure annoyed Joe. Conversation between them lagged.

Lord, You know I have something important to say to Michelle. But I guess this isn't the time or place. He knew of the perfect place to take her after dinner and addressed himself to his steak. Michelle surprised him by partaking in the dessert bar, making a small sundae with soft-serve ice cream and chocolate sprinkles. Less than an hour later, they headed out the door.

They drove down Main Street, which was still humming with the fair in full swing. Michelle stared out the window, hunkered down as if she might slide off the seat if not strapped in, a picture of relaxed contentment. "I thought you said things closed down here on Saturday nights."

"Except during Odyssey Days. They'll have fireworks after dark and then close down." He glanced at Michelle. "Do you want to watch the fireworks?"

She shook her head and sank back against the seat, her eyes closed.

"Are you all right? Do you need to go to the castle?" He

hoped she would say no. He had pinned so many dreams on talking with her tonight.

"I'll be all right." She popped her eyes open and straightened in her seat. "Where are we headed?"

"We're almost there." The spot he was headed to had a reputation as the local Lover's Lane, not that he would tell Michelle. He chose it for its natural beauty, a place he often retreated to when thinking things through.

A small park—two cement tables with a small play set—nestled under towering ponderosa pines, a creek swollen with recent summer rains rushing by. He fished an old quilt from the back of his truck and led them to the creek bank.

Michelle sat on the quilt with him, leaning her back against his chest. He resisted the temptation to kiss her, knowing it would distract from the importance of what he had to say. He settled for skimming his hands over Michelle's hair. It shimmered like gold, soft as silk. Against his will, he lifted a strand to his lips and kissed it. Michelle shivered, and his hands dropped to her shoulders. "Your muscles are bunched up." He massaged her back. As he continued to work his hands, she relaxed, some of the exhaustion he noticed in her earlier draining away.

Ever-present doves hopped closer, hoping for the food crumbs humans often scattered about them. A few ducks paddled downriver, green-banded males accompanied by sedate brown females. High in the trees lark buntings called to each other, a song of joy unlike any other. In the west the sun sank low in the sky, melding turquoise blue and brilliant gold.

"All nature sings of God," Michelle said. "It's beautiful here."

Not as beautiful as you. But Joe didn't voice his thought, afraid it might sound blasphemous, although Michelle was a work of God as much as their beautiful surroundings. "This is where I come when I want to make decisions. I sense God's presence here. Mortal flesh keeps silence while nature testifies to God."

"I can see why."

It was time. "At the fair today everyone was curious about you. Who you were, why you were with me."

Michelle giggled. "I noticed. I wouldn't be surprised to find my face plastered on the front page of the newspaper with a headline, 'Outsider Defies Tradition in Pie Contest.'"

"They wouldn't go that far," Joe said. "But I was wondering the same thing. Why were you with me?"

Michelle shifted in his arms so that she could look at his face. Cupping his face in her hands, she said, "Because I love you."

Her simple words took Joe's breath away. He longed to lean forward to take the kiss that she offered, but not yet. He had another question to ask.

"Then would you marry me? Build a life with me in Ulysses?"

fifteen

Michelle froze in Joe's arms, her mouth moving but no words coming out. She didn't know what to say. Long seconds passed.

"Did I offend you?"

"Of course not." But she shifted away from him by half an inch. Standing, he moved to the creek bank and tossed stones in the water.

Michelle joined Joe beneath a tall blue spruce. He gazed into the sky as if the stars held the answer to the mysteries of life. What must he think of her? He had offered her his most precious gift—his heart—and she had set it aside as unimportant.

"I guess I have your answer." He spoke without turning around.

The bleak note in his voice brought tears to Michelle's eyes, but she blinked them away. She had to explain, somehow. "Sit down, please." She sat on the blanket, and after a moment he joined her. "I do love you, Joe." Her voice was so quiet that she wondered if he could hear her.

"You have a funny way of showing it." He shifted to create more space between them.

"It's not you. It's, well, complicated."

He twisted around and stared her in the face. "What does that have to do with it?"

"You asked me if I wanted to build a life with you in Ulysses. But I just started the job in Denver, and. . .I need to succeed. I spread my wings and went to Romania. It was the right thing to do at the time, but now it's time for me to take care of my responsibilities. And God led me to the perfect job. I can't just up and leave it."

"So, what, you refuse to consider moving?"

"As much as I like you, Joe—I need more time. To get settled." She drew in a shaky breath. "We've known each other for less than a month. There's no need to rush."

"You seemed to enjoy yourself today. Like you belong here already." He spread his hands apart.

"I did. It was marvelous, the way a vacation is wonderful fun. Maybe I'm wrong, but I just feel like I'm supposed to stay at Mercury." Could they find a compromise, somewhere in the middle? "Do you ever think about moving back to Denver? Better opportunities for your wonderful store."

"No." Joe shook his head. "You went to Romania to spread your wings. I went to Denver. It was—okay—while it lasted, but the time came when I had to take care of my responsibilities to my family. Mum needs me."

Michelle's heart lurched. "I understand." She reached for his hand, and this time he didn't pull away. "What are we going to do?"

"Wait things out? Ask God? If we're meant for each other, we'll find the answers." He drew a deep breath that sounded like it hurt him. "I just don't like having to wait."

They both ran out of words to say and left the creek by common consent. Once in the truck, Michelle leaned out the window, feeling like Juliet waiting for Romeo to appear. Only her Romeo wouldn't come. Shaken by the turn the evening had taken, she parted from Joe with a peck on the cheek.

Later, high in her tower, Michelle longed to accept Joe's proposal with all of her heart. High above it all, she could believe true love conquered all obstacles. But down there—in the real world where she had to balance checkbooks and pay bills—it was difficult. She closed the shutters and curled up on the bed, half wishing she had her favorite teddy bear for company.

"God, if You're going to put Joe and me together, You'll have to make the way. Show me if I'm supposed to move. Or if he is."

Be still, and know that I am God. The familiar verse from Psalms came to her. She relaxed, peaceful in the arms of God's love, and fell into a restful sleep.

&

Joe paced the floor of his living room, hands clenched into tight fists curled at his side. Gawain followed his every footfall. He whined, as if wondering what had upset his master so.

The familiar household objects didn't bring their usual pleasure without someone to share them with. Michelle was the one for him—Joe knew it. God wouldn't bring two people together that way, meeting in downtown Denver of all places, only to have them go their separate ways. She could find work here, if she was willing to look.

Gawain whined again, and the two of them went out for a brief run in the dark. Joe needed to find something to take his mind off the impasse with Michelle, and he stopped by the store. Lately he'd seen brisk sales, including two of the pricey wood-carver's figurines. Buyers had snatched up all the paintings. *Sonia.* He punched in the number from memory.

"Hello?" a groggy voice answered.

"Sonia, it's me, Joe. How soon can you get that painting to me?"

"Joe?" He heard muffled sounds through the receiver. "Do you have any idea what time it is?"

A glance at the clock showed midnight. "I'm sorry. Look,

I'll call back later."

"No. That's okay. What's wrong?"

"Nothing."

"I don't believe you."

"I don't want to talk about it." She deserved a modicum of honesty. "It's personal."

"Girl trouble, huh?"

Did all women have the ability to read minds? "Kind of."

"Uh-huh."

The need to confide in someone overrode his misgivings. "I asked Michelle to marry me tonight."

"But you've only known her—" Sonia's voice sharpened.

"Three weeks. You don't have to worry. She said she wasn't sure."

Sonia didn't speak. He felt her hurt leaping across the invisible wires, and he wondered if he had made a mistake. "I guess you'll look for someone else to handle your painting now."

"Nonsense." Sonia used a brisk, business tone. "We'll always be friends." They made arrangements to ship the painting and disconnected.

I've got both the women in my life upset with me. Great going, Joe. In the back of his mind, he had always counted on Sonia, even after they broke up. On the heels of Michelle's rejection, he wondered why he ever let Sonia go. The truth was, plain and simple, he loved Michelle like he had never loved Sonia.

Joe struggled to stay awake during the pastor's sermon in church the next morning. It lacked its usual punch, at least it seemed to after the night of sleepless heartache Joe had spent. Three cups of strong coffee helped, but even so the hen scratches he used to take sermon notes looked worse than a doctor's handwriting. He rubbed his eyes again, as if that could eliminate the sandpapered, red-eye feeling.

Michelle sat beside him, their sides touching in a pew crowded with his family. She was infinitely desirable in a pink floral sundress with wide straps and a flared skirt. She seemed at ease. Did last night mean so little to her? He hoped to talk with her in private before she left, if he could find a time during Sunday dinner at the castle.

Joe wrenched his attention back to the pastor's sermon. After an agonizing twenty minutes that felt more like three hours, the organist played the chords of the closing hymn. He headed for the back door, but his hopes for a quick escape faded as everyone who hadn't met Michelle at Odyssey Days crowded in. No one seemed to notice the tension simmering between him and Michelle. She threw herself into the swarm, pumping hands, calling greetings to people she had met on the previous day. By the time they made it past the preacher at the front door, his mother and Brian's family had left.

As soon as they stepped outside, heat triggered a torrent of sweat down his back, but Michelle still looked cool. She moved with such grace, a figure skater on dry ground. She even made climbing into the cab of his truck a work of art. A lift of a leg, a swoosh of skirt, and she sat enthroned on the passenger side.

She seemed so at ease that when he climbed in beside her, he was surprised to see the flush on her face. Concern swallowed up the uncertainty of the night. "Are you feeling all right?"

෨

Michelle didn't answer. She couldn't. If she opened her mouth, she might throw up. Somehow she had survived the morning service. How she would get through an afternoon's chitchat and the drive back to Denver, she didn't know.

"Michelle?" Joe's hand felt cool against her arm.

"I'm feeling sick." She threw open the door and heaved half her breakfast on the ground.

sixteen

The heaving stopped, but the truck's low rumble set waves tossing in Michelle's stomach.

Joe was on his cell phone. "—meet you at the clinic." He folded up the instrument. "I called Brian. His clinic is about five minutes away."

"Don't suppose you have a bucket in here."

He glanced at her, and she forced a smile. She threw up twice more before they reached the clinic.

Judy waited for them at the door. Nel's presence surprised Michelle. She settled with the two girls in the waiting room.

"You didn't have to come." Michelle Morris, a three-ring circus all by herself. Bile rose in her throat, and she swayed.

"Come on back." Judy ushered Michelle to an examining room. She checked her temperature and blood pressure, making notes on a standard medical form.

"Do I have a fever?" Michelle asked.

"It's slightly elevated." Judy frowned at the thermometer.

Brian walked in. "What seems to be the problem?" Concern flooded his eyes, so like Joe's. A doctor seeing her on a Sunday—how kind they all were.

"I've been nauseated all morning. And I have this pain in my abdomen."

"Where?"

"Down here." She pointed to the right, below her navel.

"Throw up anything?"

"Three times since church ended. Oh, and a tiny bit last night." She had blamed the nausea on the unsettling

127

conversation with Joe.

"Okay. Here's what we're going to do. We'll run a CBC and a urinalysis, but we won't get the results back until tomorrow. So for now we'll start an IV, give you some fluids. . . . You'll feel better, and we'll be set up if you need more aggressive treatment later." He flashed a smile at her reaction. "I confess, I'm being overly cautious. I want to take good care of you."

Fear jumped down Michelle's tender throat. Judy had already set up the lab tray. The assortment of needles scared her more than a gun to her head at that point.

"I want to rule out infection. Based on your pain and symptoms, you could have appendicitis, so I want to monitor you closely. Although I suspect you may just have the flu. We'll give you something for the nausea with the IV." He looked over his notes at her. "If your symptoms don't improve, you'd better plan on spending another night."

"Spend the night?" Michelle gulped. "But I have to be at work in the morning. In—" Before she could get out "Denver," she had bent over, heaving again.

"You're not going anywhere like that." He looked ready to lock her in if necessary.

Michelle had something else on her mind. "I need the bathroom." She sat on the stool in misery. She hadn't felt this sick since, well, since the last time she'd had the flu. Of all the bad timing.

A knock sounded on the door. "Do you need help?" Judy's voice asked.

"Just a minute." Michelle heaved again but didn't produce much. She struggled to her feet and opened the door.

"Do you feel up to walking? We have one hospital bed here for times like this, and you'd be more comfortable."

"I'll try."

Judy led her down the hall and helped her into a hospital gown. "Nel will wash your clothes." She nodded at the spot where Michelle had soiled her garment. After she lay down, Judy reached for her hand and wrapped a tourniquet around her elbow. Michelle looked away. She didn't mind getting stuck nearly so much if she didn't watch.

After a discreet knock, Brian reentered the room. "If your fever spikes or the pain worsens, I'll run further tests. But for now I suspect you just need to wait it out."

"All right." *Be still, and know.* God reminded her of His promise the previous evening. She closed her eyes as the needle pierced the vein in her hand. *This isn't what I expected when I came to Ulysses. Not at all.* The IV made shifting positions impossible. The cool saline solution dripped into her body, soothing her and relieving some of the dryness in her throat, but not all. "May I have some water?"

"Sorry, no. NPO. That's medical jargon for nothing by mouth. Give it a few minutes, and the IV should take care of it."

Michelle told herself she wasn't hungry, and the IV did take care of most of her thirst. Even the thought of mashed potatoes made her nauseous. "Where's a basin?"

Judy rushed to her side. "Steady, steady." She grabbed a basin, and Michelle spilled brown bile. With a needle, Judy drew medicine from a bottle and squirted it into the IV. "That's for the nausea. You should feel better soon."

She laid back, too weak to argue.

"Joe and Nel are anxious to see you. Feel up to company?"

"Yes." She blurted the word. She didn't want to be left alone in this unfamiliar, uncomfortable room.

"I'll send them in, then."

❧

In the waiting room, Brian, Joe, and Nel made plans. Doctor's calls had interrupted other Sunday dinners, but rarely did the entire family get involved with the patient's care.

"I'd like to keep her here. Easier than transporting all the equipment to the castle," Brian said. "I suspect this won't last much longer."

"I'll take the girls with me, then, and come back later with supper for you. Joe, do you need anything else?"

Joe shook his head. Worry for Michelle occupied his mind. An idea jumped out. "Yeah, see if you can find some flowers."

"That will be nice. I'll be back later." Nel slipped out the door.

Judy came in. "She's resting more comfortably now and asking for company."

"I'll go in." Unlike his physician brother, Joe felt uneasy in hospital-like settings. They reminded him too forcefully of his father's final days. He opened the door to the examining room and fought the urge to flee the scene of sickness. Michelle looked so fragile, her slight figure covered with a light blanket, the IV tube trailing from her hand like an oversized earthworm. He couldn't let Michelle sense his fear. With a purposeful swagger to his walk, he crossed the room, grabbed a chair, and sat next to Michelle. "You gave me a fright there."

"Me, too. I'm so sorry. I didn't mean for our weekend to end like this."

"You know what they say, in sickness and in health." When he realized what he had said, he colored. He hadn't meant to bring up marriage. "If anyone's sorry, it's me. You're stuck here with strangers." He took her free hand with his. "Except for me, of course."

"You're all I need." A renewal of a warm current sparked between them, erasing some of the pain of the previous night's impasse. Joe didn't know the answer to their dilemma, but they would find it, somehow.

Judy knocked and came in. She took Michelle's temperature and blood pressure. "No change. Brian and I will check on you regularly."

"How long?" Michelle asked faintly.

"Brian wants to keep you all night."

"Can I help?" Joe asked.

"Check her temperature, maybe. Let me ask Brian." Judy checked Michelle's pulse. "Are you feeling better?"

"The nausea has subsided a little."

Joe stayed by Michelle's side until Nel returned later, insisting that he take time to eat. She handed him a bouquet of flowers—brilliant yellow and pink daisies. "Thank you." Judy found him a drinking glass to use as a vase, and he set it down on the cabinet next to Michelle.

"Oh, they're beautiful. Thank you." She found the strength to sit up and smell them before sinking back.

The afternoon passed slowly, Michelle drifting in and out of sleep with an occasional attempt to empty her stomach. Not much came out.

Late in the day, Brian checked on her while Michelle slept. "You should go home and get some sleep yourself. She's not in any immediate danger."

"I want to stay with Michelle." Even with her silken hair matted and tangled from a day on her back, blue veins throbbing beneath her paler-than-usual skin, lips cracked and dry, she was beautiful, at least to him. He wanted to offer her any comfort he could.

"You love her, don't you." Brian made it a statement, not a question.

"Yeah, I do." The blanket slipped from Michelle's shoulders, and Joe pulled it up. He stared at her, drinking in her loveliness, wishing their unresolved differences would go away.

"But something's wrong?" Brian probed.

"Yeah. She's got financial problems."

"Don't we all," Brian said.

"And she thinks that job in Denver is God's answer to her prayers. Ulysses is off her radar, at least for the time being."

"That's tough." The two of them looked at the sleeping woman. "It's a pity to wake her up, but I need to check her temperature again."

Michelle roused enough to take the thermometer in her mouth, smiling a bit as it slipped in, then fell back asleep.

"It's gone down a little. Sure I can't convince you to leave?" Joe shook his head.

After Brian left, Joe prayed. "Lord, I know You have a purpose in this. I confess I'm full of fears, and I know they don't make much sense. Michelle isn't Dad, but I don't like seeing her so sick. And what will she do if she misses work and can't pay her bills?"

There is no fear in love. But perfect love drives out fear.

I know, Lord. Help me to love her more perfectly. Driven by an inner impulse, he hunted for the Bible Brian kept in the waiting room and began reading the Psalms.

🔖

Michelle didn't wake until the setting sun blazed through the west window, its warmth burrowing through the thin blanket. Joe occupied a seat to her right, an open Bible on his lap.

Joe's still here. Had he ever left? She shifted as much as the IV would allow and studied his achingly familiar profile. The sunset transformed his brown hair into copper and shaded his face a golden bronze. Waking to find him at her side made her feel cherished.

He looked up from what he was reading. "Good. You're awake. How are you feeling?"

"A little better. Still as weak as a newborn kitten. Is that a Bible you're reading?"

Joe nodded. "I've discovered some super things this afternoon." Enthusiasm leapt through his voice.

"What's that?"

"God reminded me that perfect love drives out fear. So I started looking for verses about love. I've found so many references to love in the Psalms, I stopped counting them. And not one of them is about the love between a man and a woman. How about this one." He flipped back a few pages. " 'Show me the wonders of your great love, you who save by your right hand those who take refuge in you from their foes.'" He scanned down the page. "Or this one: 'For the king trusts in the Lord; through the unfailing love of the Most High he will not be shaken.'" He continued turning pages and reading verses for several minutes.

Michelle smiled, basking in the warmth of his enthusiasm, the exuberance of a man emptying his toolbox in search of the perfect tool. She let the words flow over her, recognizing a familiar verse here and there.

He took her hand in his. "The only perfect love is God's love, of course. But our answer is here, in His word. I know it is. We just have to find it." His face beamed with the satisfaction of a child who had solved a difficult problem.

If only it could be that simple. What will happen if I can't go to work in the morning? She didn't qualify for sick days, not until she had been on the job for three months. "I know, Joe. But the answers have to make their way from my head to my heart."

Joe's face fell. Michelle hated to hurt him. "You're right. God will give us the answers, if we ask Him for wisdom. Give me my Bible, please." She pointed to where it lay next to her purse in the corner.

They read the Bible together all evening, finishing the Psalms then utilizing the concordance in the back of

Michelle's Bible to find other verses about God's love. The study absorbed their attention, and queasiness bothered Michelle less and less. They hardly noticed Brian's comings and goings.

The sky outside the window turned black, and Brian came in. "Lights out. You need to go home, little brother. That's an order."

"I didn't realize it was so late." Joe ran his hand through his hair, creating uneven waves. He leaned over and kissed Michelle on the cheek. "I'll be back first thing in the morning."

Michelle didn't ask if she could leave. She no longer felt sick, but she knew she was too weak to leave in her condition. Hopefully in the morning.

Joe left, and Brian turned off the lights. "Judy and I will continue to check on you throughout the night. I can't promise you uninterrupted rest." She laughed with him, and he left.

She was alone in the unfriendly room. She missed Joe already. The verses they had read from 1 Corinthians 13 reverberated like a refrain in her head. *Love always protects, always trusts, always hopes, always perseveres.* The uncomfortable bed, the unfriendly environment of white and steel, faded in its rhythm, lulling her to sleep.

When she awoke early the next morning, she saw Brian sitting spread-eagled on a rolling stool. "How do you feel?"

"Much better."

"Glad to hear it." He smiled. "How does breakfast sound?"

"Wonderful." Michelle was ravenous.

"Mother will be here soon with food and clean clothes. And Judy will take out the IV. You should be set to go within the hour."

Michelle glanced at the clock. She wouldn't get on the

road until almost eight, the hour she was supposed to be at the office. Nothing she could do about it, however.

Judy busied herself removing the needle from Michelle's hand. "Keep pressure on it." She placed a gauze pad on the puncture point.

"You're a good nurse. I hardly felt a thing."

"I wish I got to do it all the time. I spend half my time out front, scheduling patients, answering the phone."

Michelle cocked her head and looked at the couple. Might as well offer them the benefit of her human resources expertise. "Are you busy enough to hire an office manager?"

"Probably." Brian beat the pen on the clipboard. "In fact, that's a great idea. Are you interested in the job?"

seventeen

Before Michelle could answer, Joe and Nel entered the room. The aromas of hot coffee, sizzling bacon, and maple syrup filled the air, and Michelle's mouth watered.

"I brought you some breakfast, dear. Brian called to say you would probably be hungry this morning." Without fuss Nel arranged a plate and cups brimming with juice and coffee on the tray.

"Good morning. Feeling better?" Joe limited himself to a kiss on Michelle's cheek and handed over her overnight bag. "Mother washed your clothes last night. Brian has a shower here, or you can go back to the castle if you'd like."

Michelle looked at the circle surrounding her, all concerned for her welfare, and felt loved and part of a family that wasn't even hers. They had all been so kind. An hour later, showered, dressed, and fed, Michelle walked to her car, Joe by her side. He held her hand, their arms swinging slightly in a comfortable rhythm.

"I'd better call my boss. I'm an hour late for work already." Michelle dialed Chavonne's extension. She didn't answer. More worried than ever, she redialed the main number, and the operator connected her with Glenda Harris.

"Hello?"

Michelle heard the vice president's crisp tones, and her throat constricted. How could she explain her emergency to the supervisor, who gave the impression that she had no heart? But Michelle had to try.

"Miss Harris, this is Michelle Morris. I was calling to tell you I will be late today. I should be there in a couple of hours. I was sick—"

The woman on the other end didn't give her the opportunity to explain. "Michelle Morris. Didn't you just start working at Mercury?"

"Yes, two weeks ago—"

"And you couldn't call last night to let Miss Walker know?"

"I was too sick, hooked up to an IV—"

"We expect our employees—"

Was it Michelle's imagination, or did Miss Harris emphasize those words?

"—to keep us informed and to work their shifts except in the case of emergencies." Her voice held a severe reprimand.

"I'm sorry. I was sick." The words came out squeaky and uncertain. *I had an emergency. I couldn't help it. If I hadn't gone to Ulysses, I'd probably be at work by now.* Anger fought with humiliation, leaving her shaken.

"I'll make a note in your file. I'll let Miss Walker know that you will be in at noon today." The phone clicked in her ear.

Michelle didn't know what to make of the conversation. Had she been threatened?

"She was rough on you." Joe must have sensed her unspoken worry. "I'm sorry this had to happen, even if it meant I got to spend extra time with you. I'm glad you're doing better now." His fingers brushed a stray strand of hair from her cheek. "Quite a weekend, huh? Not what you expected when you came to Ulysses."

"Not exactly." She clenched her teeth against the acid in her throat. *Perfect love casts out fear*, she reminded herself, and it subsided.

"Willing to give it another try? Look at it this way. It can't be worse than this weekend." His smile could melt ice cream, and before Michelle thought about it, she agreed to return to Ulysses soon.

The following Friday, Sonia's painting arrived at Joe's store without a hitch. In spite of his eagerness to view the work, he took his time opening the packaging, cutting the box ends with an X-Acto knife, and turning the frame with each layer of bubble wrap until the bright colors shimmered into view.

The power of the painting stunned him. Sonia had darkened the shadows on the valley side, sharpening the contrast with the bright colors of the garden that drew the eye to the light of the passage through the mountains. Her best work yet, it wouldn't look out of place in a museum.

He hung it on the back wall and fiddled with lighting to provide the right illumination. Finished, he poured a cup of coffee and studied its effect. The thrill of bringing great art to the public rushed through him. A part of him hoped he could keep it in his shop for a few weeks so as many people as possible could enjoy it with him. But that was impractical, and what was more, he had already contacted a potential buyer who was eager to see the painting firsthand.

Someone rang the doorbell. Stanford Dixon, a local lawyer who had built a career of defending DWUIs into a thriving criminal practice, had arrived. He was a Christian, and one of Joe's best customers. Setting down his coffee cup, he opened the front door. "Good morning, Stan."

"Is it here? I saw the truck." Before Joe could answer, Stan caught sight of the painting on the wall. He studied it without speaking for several moments, cocking his head this way and peering closely at different areas of canvas. He stepped back and made rectangular shapes with his hands, as if envisioning it on the wall of his office.

"You didn't do it justice. It's magnificent. You were right— this is one I have to have. A visual reminder for my clients that there's always light at the end of the tunnel."

Did all lawyers speak in clichés?

Stan whipped out his checkbook and wrote a check for the agreed-upon amount with a business-boosting number of zeros. "I'm having my office remodeled. Can you keep it here until then?"

Better than expected.

"I'd be happy to." Joe kept his enthusiasm in check. "I was just thinking it would look good in a museum."

"So that someone else besides my clients could see it?" Stan jabbed Joe in the ribs.

Now that you mention it, yes. "I was thinking about the larger number of people. No harm in dreaming big."

"You can't keep them all."

Although Joe couldn't understand why someone wanted to defend drunk drivers, Stan was a good sort, and he could afford the more pricey pieces. He wandered through the store, studying the new displays with calculating eyes. "Most of this is new."

"I had a successful run through Odyssey Days, had to put out new stuff."

"This is lovely." He admired dawn-gold blown glass, reached out his hands as if to touch, then stuffed them in his pockets. "Maybe another time."

After he left, Joe picked up his phone and dialed Sonia. "He bought it for the amount we expected. A little more, in fact."

"Great." The phone whined in his ear, and he pictured her dancing a jig in her excitement. "Can we get together for a celebration dinner? My treat?"

Go to Denver. Why not? See Michelle again. A flush of shame washed over him. Sonia had invited him, and the first person he thought of was Michelle. "Better wait until the check clears."

Sonia chuckled at the old joke. The first time Joe

represented one of Sonia's pieces, the buyer gave him a check and left with the time-consuming project. The check bounced, and he never recovered the fee, although he reimbursed Sonia. Once stung, doubly careful. That buyer came from Denver. "I'll call the next time I'm in Denver."

"To see Michelle, I suppose. Not that it's any of my business. When do you think that will be?"

Joe regretted accepting her invitation to dinner. "I don't know. I haven't decided."

"Well, thanks for finding me a buyer." The conversation ended on an uncomfortable note.

Joe walked around the store, studying the balance of the display with the big painting in place. He decided he needed to move the abstract painting that Michelle had accused of giving her headaches farther away from Sonia's work and to hang the painting of the Maroon Bells that Michelle had liked so well there instead. While he straightened objects and adjusted their positions, he gave serious thought about going back to Denver.

Maybe he should consider opening a branch store in the capital. He knew a real estate agent who could help him find a reasonably priced rental, and of course, he would turn the day-to-day operation over to a manager. But even so, he would need to spend a lot of time in the city, especially at first. And he had made a promise to himself and to his family to stay nearby.

Face it, Joe. The only reason you're thinking about branching out is because of Michelle. He had thought about opening a second store someday, but not yet.

Perfect love casts out fear. He resolved to check into store sites the next time he went to Denver. Both he and Michelle would have to compromise if things were ever going to work out between them.

❧

The rest of the week passed smoothly for Michelle. Upon her arrival at work on Monday, Chavonne had inquired after her health, and Michelle's worries subsided. She must have caught some kind of twenty-four-hour bug.

Carrie, on the other hand, appeared to catch whatever bug Michelle had. She was sick every morning and didn't make it out of bed before Michelle left for work. Saturday was their first real chance to talk since Michelle's return from Ulysses.

"I know what made you sick last weekend." Carrie nibbled on a cracker and washed it down with hot tea.

"A flu bug, that's what."

"No, I think it was something else. You weren't in love when you were in Romania—only in love with the idea of love. Things are different now." Carrie grinned to let Michelle know she was teasing.

"I wish." Michelle didn't argue with Carrie using the word *love*. "Joe asked me to marry him on Saturday night."

"What?" The cracker broke in half in Carrie's hand. "And you're just telling me this now?"

Michelle squirmed. "I wasn't ready to share it."

"You don't seem happy about it." Carrie dabbed a bit of jelly on the cracker. "What did you tell him?"

"That God provided this job for me in Denver, and I have responsibilities I have to take care of. It's like the timing is all wrong." She stuffed a cracker in her mouth, mashed down on it once, and swallowed hard. "If only Joe lived in Denver."

Carrie's face paled, and she crunched crackers and sipped tea until color returned to her face. "We both know as well as anyone that it's useless to live our lives on the basis of what-ifs and if-onlys and whys. If God had let me adopt Viktor when I wanted to, I might never have fallen in love with Steve. And there's more." She clasped her hands protectively over her abdomen. Dark circles under her friend's eyes underlined the pallor that had settled on her skin, and tired lines around her eyes made her look older than her years.

She's—

"I'm pregnant."

"Congratulations!" Michelle reached to hug Carrie but stopped short when her friend didn't seem as thrilled as she expected.

"Frankly, I'm a little scared. I saw what happened to Lila. Steve's first wife, you know. I was there when she died."

"There's no reason to think you'll have the same problems. And you'll be here in Denver, with first-class medical care."

"You're right. But the fear is still there. Steve, too, although he tries to hide it for my sake."

Michelle didn't know what to say. If she were in Carrie's shoes, she'd probably feel the same way.

"We didn't plan on having a baby right now. I wanted to work for a few years, and I am a little afraid. We could let our concerns control us. We could have decided never to have children, for instance. Or I could spend my 'confinement' in bed like an invalid—as it is, Steve coddles me. But we love each other, and we trust God to take care of me and the baby. And the timing. That's the bottom line. Going ahead, trusting in God's goodness, even when we don't understand it." She wrapped the stack of crackers back in the packaging and put it back in the box. "The morning I found out for sure, I read a terrific quote in my devotional book. Something about 'exercise your faith' and 'be not detained by self-doubt.' I think about that when I get a little scared."

That makes sense. Maybe Michelle should consider Brian's job offer. She shook her head. No, she didn't doubt God's leading to her job. Maybe God would convince Joe to open a store in Denver.

eighteen

Joe rolled down his truck window. He enjoyed the sensation of wind whipping through his hair, singing at the top of his lungs, the air rushing by swallowing up his voice. "Oh, what a beautiful morning." Not a cloud marred the bright blue sky, and nothing shadowed the asphalt that shimmered ahead like black crystals sprinkled in a straight line as far as the eye could see.

"I've got a beautiful feeling." *Michelle, Michelle.* His heart sang in rhythm with the rolling wheels. He had decided to make a short trip to Denver and drop in on Michelle unannounced.

She should be pleased to see me again in Denver. If not for Michelle, he would never have discussed the idea with Mum, and she would never have said to go for it.

Mile after mile of growing crops undulated in the light wind, the "amber waves of grain" immortalized by Katharine Lee Bates in "America the Beautiful." He pulled over at a historical site marker and read a panel about the Kansas Pacific Railroad. Taking a swig from his water bottle, he breathed in the scents of sweet-smelling hay and the moist earth, saying good-bye to the plains before the mountains appeared over the next ridge. He enjoyed the Rockies, but the plains gave him a feeling of serenity and continuity, endless variations of yellow and green and brown with an occasional splash of bright color.

His watch chimed, reminding him of the hour, and he jumped in the truck. He hoped to catch Michelle when she left work. The thought of seeing her again made his heart beat faster and his foot press down harder on the accelerator. The truck spurted forward.

The mountains climbed into view, snow still visible on the highest peaks on this clear August day. Colorado had the best of all worlds.

Soon the outskirts of Denver came into view. He slipped off the highway to avoid the rush-hour gridlock and wound his way downtown, arriving at Mercury Communications at five o'clock on the dot.

Employees left the building two or three at a time, but he didn't see Michelle. At quarter past, he was puzzled, and at five thirty he checked his watch against radio time. Impatience changed to worry after another fifteen minutes. Had he missed her somehow? He pulled out his cell phone and dialed the Romeros' number.

"Hello?" a man answered.

"Steve, this is Joe Knight. Say, has Michelle come home yet?"

"I haven't seen her." Joe heard a rustle that sounded like curtains. "Her car's not here, either. I'll tell her you called."

At that moment—precisely five minutes before six—Michelle walked out the front door.

"Don't bother. I see her." Joe closed the phone and jumped out the door. Racing to meet her, an idiotic grin on his face, he stopped a foot away from her. "Hi there, beautiful. Want a date tonight?"

"Joe." Her smile expressed her pleasure in seeing him. Her brief kiss on the lips made him shiver with delight. "What are you doing here?"

"I took advantage of some business to come to Denver. Are you free for supper?" They decided on a restaurant on the west side of town, and he escorted her to her car, pausing at the door long enough for another brief kiss.

A few minutes later they parked side by side at Gaetano's, an Italian restaurant converted from a Victorian house. The smiling waitress led them to a secluded spot. In the corner booth, Joe put his arm around Michelle while they studied the menu together. He already knew what he wanted to order, so he spent his time studying her profile. How he had missed her.

As if sensing his thoughts, she turned her head and smiled at him. "It's good to see you again."

All his reservations about opening a store in Denver fled at her smile. Surely he could find the right property, and then. . . and then Michelle would fall in his arms and marry him? Could it be that easy? He still didn't want to live in Denver, away from family, and she was committed to her job.

As soon as the waitress took their order—shrimp fra diavolo for Joe, fiorintina salad for Michelle—she started a minute-by-minute description of her activities for the week. Mercury asked her to develop training manuals for one of the departments.

"I spent Tuesday in Web Services. . . ."

She's only on Tuesday? Joe nursed his iced tea, squeezing the lemon slice for extra flavor, and inserted an appropriate comment when she paused for breath. "What's Web Services?"

She paused, as if surprised by his question, and her answer lasted through the salad course.

"After I spent Tuesday in the Web Services department, I started working on the manual today."

The waitress brought out the main course, Michelle's salad with perfectly grilled steak and Joe's shrimp over pasta.

When she talked about her job, Michelle's face came alive. Her voice sped up like a tape on fast forward, high-pitched but clearly enunciated. He was excited because she was excited.

She hasn't asked about my store, my family, once. Joe wanted to ignore the thought as unfair and selfish, but it wouldn't go away.

"So you still haven't told me why you're in Denver." Michelle forked a bite of mushroom, artichoke, and steak and brought it to her mouth and chewed it thoughtfully.

You didn't give me a chance.

"Did you have business with one of the artists you met at the arts festival? Sonia?"

Joe caught a hint of jealousy behind the neutral question. *Maybe that's why she didn't ask. Afraid I came here to see Sonia.*

"No." He raised his glass in a mock toast. "Here's to Trojan Horse II, to open in Denver in the near future."

"Why, that's wonderful." The instantaneous smile lit Michelle's face like a sunrise.

"Yeah, I talked it over with Mum. Business has been going well lately, and I can afford to expand. Provided, of course, that I can find the right spot. Opening a store in Denver is bound to cost more than it does in Ulysses, and then there's the matter of inventory."

"It will be a terrific success. I know it will." Her eyes lost their glazed-over tiredness, and she turned serious. "Thanks for giving it a try. It means a lot to me." She took a drink of water. "Anyhow, let me know if there's anything I can do to help."

The evening ended soon after that, Michelle pleading the need for an early start in the morning. They made plans for dinner the next night.

The next day, as Joe paged through the commercial real estate section of the newspaper, he remembered her offer. He wished Michelle could spend the day with him, for her companionship if nothing else. He suspected she didn't have much experience in commercial rentals. He had an appointment with a Realtor that afternoon, but he figured there was no harm in checking what the paper had to offer.

With a Denver map spread before him, he circled those areas that interested him most and crossed out the areas he wanted to avoid. He doubted neighborhoods had changed much since he had moved away, but he would check with the local police station before he rented anything in any case.

One by one he evaluated the listings in the morning paper. He dismissed the ones that said "charming"—which could mean anything from "small" to "antique"—as well as ones that read "fixer-upper." He didn't want to have to reinvent the wheel. Some neighborhoods were just too pricey. In the end he marked four possibilities. *No time like the present.* A message at the first number he dialed gave the address. A quick glance at the map confirmed it was located in a bad area.

The next listing had already rented, and the third cost enough to bankrupt Fort Knox. That left the final listing, on the small side according to the square footage but a possibility depending on the arrangement of the rooms. He consumed a lonely sandwich and sought out the rental property. When he spotted an art gallery across the street, he decided against pursuing it.

The Realtor he met in the afternoon took his information but cautioned him he might not find an acceptable property in his price range. By dinnertime the hours of fruitless searching had taken their toll. Joe cheered himself up with thoughts of dinner with Michelle. After a brief stop at the hotel to freshen up, he drove to Carrie's house. Traffic everywhere in Denver seemed heavy these days, and the trip took longer than he expected.

When he arrived, he saw Steve playing catch with Viktor. Steve spotted him. "Hi there. Go on in." He passed the ball to the boy, and once again their play absorbed their attention. Joe wished he had a home like this to come to, with a wife and child waiting. He hurried up the steps.

Carrie met him at the door, wiping her hands on her apron. "Michelle called. She's trying to finish a project to show to her boss tomorrow. She said she'll be home by seven, eight at the latest. She told me to take care of you. Do you want to eat with us?"

Joe considered refusing, but he had eaten his lonely lunch hours ago, and he wasn't sure when he and Michelle would eat. "Sure." He headed back to the front door. "I'll hang out with the guys for a while."

"Great." Carrie flashed a smile in his direction as she stirred something on the stove.

Joe went back outside. "Mind if I join you?"

"Sure. If you'll catch, Viktor can bat the ball." He high-fived his son, who disappeared into the garage and reappeared with a plastic bat. "Let's go into the backyard."

"Nerf baseball?" Joe smiled.

"I have a softball when we can get to the park. Here we play it safe. Don't want any broken windows. Batter up."

Viktor took his place behind an old couch pillow that served as home plate. Joe crouched down behind the boy. He got in a day's worth of exercise chasing foul balls and Steve's pitches. By the time Carrie called them in to supper, he felt reenergized.

The meal was simple, spaghetti with salad. He sipped his iced tea, brewed, not instant—the way he liked it. He had never tasted Michelle's cooking, unless he counted the scones she made with his mother. He wondered if she existed on microwave dinners and restaurant dining, with an occasional home-cooked meal at a friend's house. He knew so little about her day-to-day life.

They finished eating, and Joe retired to the den with

Steve while Carrie gave Viktor a bath. Steve turned on the television to a Rockies' game at seven. Michelle still hadn't arrived. *I hope she gets here soon.*

&

Michelle left the office at eight p.m. With traffic moving close to the posted speed limit, she made it home in a short fifteen minutes. Today's shift left her more drained than anything since some of her longer days in Romania.

Joe's blue pickup sat in front of the house. *I had almost forgotten him.* Her heart lifted, and a new boost of energy removed some of the tiredness. She walked in the house with a lighthearted step. Carrie greeted her at the door. "Steve and I will tuck Viktor in bed, so you two can have some privacy." She hugged her friend.

Michelle found Joe in the den. "Sorry I'm so late. What a mess at work." She sank down on the sofa next to Joe and kicked off her heels. "Oh, that feels good."

Joe massaged her shoulders, his strong fingers working miracles in her tense muscles. "Bad day, was it?"

She nodded. Under half-closed eyes she murmured, "Do you mind awfully if we don't go out? I'm sure we could scare up something to eat here."

"Yeah, sure." His mouth twisted in a funny smile. "Carrie already fed me. I hope you don't mind." He withdrew his hands from her shoulders and intertwined their fingers.

"I'll get some leftovers then." Michelle laid her head on Joe's shoulder, allowing herself to relax for a few minutes without moving. The longer she waited, the less she wanted to stir herself.

Joe loosened his fingers and brushed her hair back from her forehead. "I'll go fix something for you." He stood.

"No." Michelle struggled to a sitting position, but he shook his head.

"Let me." She heard the microwave door opening and closing. "Do you want coffee or tea?"

"Coffee sounds good." Maybe that would help her wake up. She had no energy left over for company tonight. *But this is Joe,* her conscience argued back. *The man whose smile makes your heart beat faster.* She got to her feet and joined him in the kitchen. "Did you have any luck today?"

"Zilch." His voice quivered with disappointment. "Nothing. Nada. Not a sniff."

The microwave chimed, and Joe brought her a bowl of spaghetti while he looked into the refrigerator. "Do you want the parmesan cheese?" He pulled out a bowl of salad and dressing.

"Sure." Parmesan might wake up her taste buds.

The coffee finished brewing, and Joe poured cups for both of them before joining her at the table. "I was hoping for some kind of lead. The Realtor didn't sound too hopeful that I could find something workable in the price range I can afford." He took a deep swig of his coffee. "And I have to return to Ulysses tomorrow."

"Go back?" The fork in Michelle's hand slipped. "But you just got here. I guess I was hoping you could at least stay through Friday night."

"Saturdays are our busiest days. I need to spend the night at home tomorrow so I can be up early Saturday."

Disappointment brought tears to the edge of Michelle's eyes. Work had robbed her of extra time with Joe tonight. She had counted on him staying in Denver through the weekend, but of course he had to be at his store.

"You are coming down for another visit this weekend, aren't you?"

Michelle remembered a vague discussion, but she had forgotten it in the press of work. "I don't know if I can. I might have to work Saturday." After missing that half day after her last visit, she had worked extra hard to prove herself. *Sorry, Ms. Harris, I made other plans?* Mercury expected commitment from its employees.

"What's so special about this job? It sounds like they work you nonstop."

Did he expect her to blow off her boss's demands in order to spend an extra day with him? He knew how important this job was to her. The pent-up frustration from the hard pace at work boiled out. She glared at Joe. "I don't understand what you have against my job."

nineteen

Joe wiped off his mouth and looked at her without blinking. "Just that it seems to always come between us. And why don't you understand that I have to be there for my mother?" He paused and took a deep breath. "I'm going to leave before I say something we'll both regret. We can talk about it later." He walked out the door without saying another word.

Go after him. Michelle struggled to rise from her chair. Discouragement and exhaustion as huge as a salmon fighting his way upstream threw her back on the couch. Nothing was going right—not with Joe, not at work. She could lose both.

Michelle put the rest of the spaghetti away without finishing it. She went to bed, but she stayed awake until well past midnight, replaying the evening in her mind. Two hours later hunger woke her up, demanding food. She slept in fits and starts for a while before heading to the kitchen for a quick snack.

She found Carrie placing banana slices on bread already slathered with peanut butter. When she saw Michelle, a surreptitious look passed over her face. "It seems morning sickness doesn't apply to the hours between midnight and five a.m. I was craving a peanut butter and banana sandwich."

Ugh. "So cravings aren't an old wives' myth." Michelle dropped a couple of slices of wheat bread in the toaster and poured a glass of juice.

"Apparently not." Carrie ran her finger around the edge of the peanut butter jar and licked it. "What's up with you?"

"Joe and I had an argument." Michelle stabbed a knife in the blueberry jam.

"That's good."

"Huh?" Michelle slathered jam over her sandwich.

"So you can learn how to resolve differences."

"Yeah right. He had a bad day. I had a bad day. And we took it out on each other. At least I think that's what happened."

"What are you going to do about it?"

"Call him, I suppose. But I'm still mad. He comes to Denver unannounced and expects me to drop everything."

"If you play a game of who's right and who's wrong, you'll both lose."

"I suppose you're right." Michelle nibbled on the toast. "I guess I could call." She reached for the phone then remembered the time. "I'd better wait a few hours, though."

The following morning, Michelle dialed Joe, but it went straight to voice mail. She frowned. Not a lot of time remained before she had to leave for work. She pressed the END button, and the phone beeped. Someone had left a message. She'd better check.

"This is Joe. Look, I'm sorry about last night. Please call me. I'll be at home until eight." His voice was ragged, as if he had slept as little as she had last night. *And it's my fault.* Her decision about the weekend was easy.

She hit the REDIAL button. Joe answered immediately.

"Michelle?" That one word expressed all of his regret and uncertainty and hope.

"Oh Joe." She stopped, unable to say any more.

"I was a jerk last night."

"No, I was out of line. I was so tired, I was only thinking of myself." Now the words came without effort. "But the solution is obvious. If I do have to work on Saturday, I'll drive down at night and come back on Sunday."

Joe's audible sigh held heartfelt relief. "That would be

great. I have to be at the store most of Saturday anyway."

"I can't wait." Michelle hung up the phone and leaned against the wall, a warm feeling brimming over in her heart.

Although she worked as hard on Friday and Saturday as earlier in the week, the effort did not exhaust her to the same level. Saturday night found her barreling down the highway toward Ulysses.

੨੦

When Joe spotted Michelle's car entering the driveway to the castle, he ran out the door, meeting her halfway across the courtyard. He greeted her with a kiss as necessary as water for a parched man home from the desert. "I've missed you."

"Me, too." They walked into the castle, hand in hand.

Joe picked at the traditional English meal of lamb chops, peas, and potatoes. He'd rather feast his eyes on Michelle. He made a point of asking her about work.

"It's been terrible. Working ten- and twelve-hour days, checking and rechecking the facts for my training manual, running a beta test on it. And after all that work, the vice president didn't like big chunks of it and asked me to rewrite it. She thinks I'm working on it this weekend." Michelle tittered. Tiny tension lines appeared around her eyes that hadn't been there before.

"You must be exhausted. Thanks for coming." Joe resolved to help Michelle release the tension accumulated during the week and shifted the conversation to other topics.

"Have some more potatoes, dear." Mum handed the serving bowl to Michelle. "I heard from the Kildaires today. I wondered if you have met them, Michelle. They're missionaries in Romania. In Constanta."

"Rick and Kim?"

His mother nodded.

"Oh yes. They ran a guesthouse where we went for a vacation. Wonderful people. How did you meet them?"

"On the Internet. I read an article about them in our church's magazine that gave their e-mail address. Their work sounded interesting. I've thought about doing something like that with our home. I wrote a brief note, and Kim kindly responded."

"As they say, it's a small world."

"Actually, I write to people all around the world. They come to our church, or I read about them, and we start corresponding. I spent a small fortune in postage before computers came of age."

"What got you interested in missions?" Michelle leaned forward, one elbow on the table.

"It started with writing to my friends in England. Later my interests expanded, and I wrote to more and more people. My husband used to joke that we could make a trip around the world and never stay in a motel. Someday I'd like to make that trip."

"It was kind of like that for me. I always loved it when a missionary came and spoke at our church."

"You and Dad did make a trip to England when we were kids. I remember wondering why you would want to travel so far from home." Joe forked a potato.

"I know you hated staying with your aunt that summer. But I find that as long as I can get away now and then, there's no place like home. Which is in Colorado with my family." His mother stood. "Dessert anyone? I have bread pudding tonight."

"I'll take some," Joe said.

Michelle, who had polished her plate, demurred. "Instant access to the entire world. When I was in Romania, all I had to do was get online. How much harder it must have been for the early missionaries who had so little contact with home for years at a time." She bent over and reached into the bag at her feet. "Speaking of Romania. . .here is the scrapbook I promised you."

"Let me clear the table."

The three of them made quick work of clearing off the dishes and wiping down the table surface. Michelle placed the scrapbook in front of Joe, and the two women sat on either side. They spent the rest of the evening talking about Michelle's experiences in Romania. Joe thought he recognized the pictures of Pastor Radu, the national pastor Michelle had worked with, and the sister in charge of the orphanage was unforgettable. Joe took the scrapbook with him when he left for the night.

৵

In the Rosebriar room, Michelle discovered a pen she thought she had lost waiting on the nightstand. *They say you only leave something behind if you want to return.* If she kept coming for visits, they'd have to change the name of the room from Rosebriar to Michelle's Kingdom. The strange castle felt more like home all the time.

After Joe left, Nel had shown Michelle her office—named the Time Portal—with its dazzling array of the latest equipment. Thinking of electronic gadgets, she owed an e-mail to her pastor in Romania. She'd neglected answering his last message in the crush at work. One more thing to add to her to-do list of tasks neglected with her new schedule.

The high-canopied bed invited Michelle to recline, and she settled in. When she awoke the next morning, she felt more refreshed than she had all week.

After the church service, Brian and Judy invited Joe and Michelle over for dinner. "Our Bible study group is getting together. We meet twice a month."

Brian and Judy's home, an understated three-bedroom brick house, was located in a new housing development. Children, including Pepper and Poppy as well as numerous others from toddlers to adolescents, swarmed around the backyard play set and trampoline like honeybees.

Michelle had met most of the adults at Odyssey Days. The men congregated in the basement, shooting pool. Michelle joined the ladies in chopping vegetables and deveining shrimp. The informal atmosphere made her feel right at home. Conversation circled around work, children, and favorite books before taking a serious turn.

"That guy who murdered the pregnant mother was on the news last night," Judy said. "Something about his appeal."

"Why can't they fry him and get it over with?" Kit, the tall, muscular deputy sheriff, said.

"The longer he lives, the more opportunity he has to repent and receive God's forgiveness." Marge, a soft-spoken elementary school teacher, said.

"Those prison conversions don't convince me," Kit said.

Sheila Classen, a school social worker, spoke up next. "Well, I think—"

"We all know how you feel about the death penalty, Sheila." Kit slapped her knife down on the table as if in disgust.

A lively discussion ensued, exploring the question of the death penalty from all sides. Michelle hadn't taken part in such a spirited debate since college. She found it easy to share her own opinions.

Moments after Brian took steaks outside to grill, Joe rushed in. "I've got to go."

"What happened?" Michelle picked up her purse.

"The sheriff called. Someone's broken into the store."

twenty

The way Joe drove, Michelle feared they might have an accident between Brian's house and downtown Ulysses. Joe must have broken every speed limit covering the three miles. Kit, the deputy, followed at a more reasonable pace. At each stop sign, he tapped the steering wheel nervously, and the car skidded through a yellow caution light. Michelle decided not to say anything until they saw the extent of the damage.

The sheriff directed them to the back door, which swung open. Joe hurried to meet him. "Have you been inside?"

"Just long enough to see there'd been a break-in." The sheriff shook his head. "I can't believe this happened. I was waiting on you and keeping guard."

Joe lunged for the door.

"Wait a sec." The sheriff dug a white handkerchief out of his pocket and pushed against the handle. "We'll have to check for any fingerprints."

Dust swirled in the shaft of light from the door, obscuring the room. After Michelle's eyes adjusted to the semidarkness, she saw construction paper and broken clay projects scattered across the floor, as if someone had brushed them off the shelves in an effort to find more profitable items. From what Michelle remembered of the inventory, she believed the thief had taken the expensive coffee table art books as well as several of the models—including the car Viktor had put together. She blinked back tears.

&

Joe ignored the damage in the studio and pushed into the

158

gallery. He stood at the door, and his shoulders sagged so low his disappointed bones could have pierced his heart.

The wood-carver's figurines—gone. Unusual blown-glass vases—gone. Numerous paintings, from pastel nature scenes to modern art—gone. He forced himself to turn to the wall where Sonia's painting had hung. The space gaped empty, as barren as Coors Field during hockey season. His hands balled at his sides. *This wasn't supposed to happen.*

Others came in behind him. Kit, who had followed them from the Bible study, checked the front door. "No sign of forced entry." She bent down to study a mark on the floor.

"We'll need a list of what was taken," the sheriff said. "You're insured, of course?"

"Yes." But the financial loss only represented a small part of the picture. Every stolen object, even a single pencil, tore a piece out of his heart.

Michelle wandered around, her face mirroring the shock he felt inside. "All those beautiful things." Tears misted her eyes.

Don't cry. Don't get me started.

Joe wheeled around on his heels and marched into the classroom. He went for a trash bag, wanting to get the destruction out of sight as soon as possible.

"Don't do that." Kit's voice was sharp. "Wait until we've finished our investigation."

But what can I do? Inwardly Joe wailed. Helplessness overpowered him. He slumped into a hard-backed chair and leaned over, his head resting between his hands.

He heard the quiet rustle of silk, and Michelle knelt on the floor next to him, her arms circling him, resting his head on her shoulder. His hurt ran too deep for words, but her presence gave him strength. In spite of his resolve, he allowed a few tears to fall. After a few minutes, they separated, their hands still wrapped together like a Gordian knot.

He drew a deep breath. "I've got to call Sonia. Her painting was the most valuable piece I had." Shaking fingers punched in her number.

"Hi, Joe. What's up?" The innocent laughter in Sonia's voice mocked his pain.

"Someone stole your painting, Sonia."

"What?"

"The store. It's been stripped clean."

"How horrible. Wait a minute." He could hear her pencil beating a rhythm against the phone. "I'll leave right away. Don't move until I get there. You're at the store?"

Joe swept his gaze across the shelves, the empty spots giving it the look of a lopsided checkerboard. "Yeah, we're here."

"An hour and a half, two hours tops. Is someone with you?"

"Michelle." He knew it might hurt.

"Good. You shouldn't be alone." She surprised him. "I'm on my way."

Joe went into his office and printed out an inventory list but found he couldn't concentrate. Time dragged while Kit and the sheriff combed the store for evidence.

Some time later, Michelle asked, "Have you let the buyer know? That lawyer."

"No." Joe punched in Dixon's phone number.

Before Joe could supply any details, Dixon cut him off. "Meet me in my office. Ten minutes."

"I—can't. I'm waiting for the artist who painted the picture."

"All the better. I'd like to meet her. And bring your insurance policy with you."

After he hung up, Michelle's hands made shooing motions. "Go on. If you're not back by the time Sonia arrives, I'll bring her over. Just tell me the address."

Outside, the street reflected the same peace and quiet that had lulled him into a false sense of security. The people of Ulysses didn't commit crimes like grand theft. A few supplies had taken flight over the years, but never anything of real value. He tried to calm his shaking insides when Dixon greeted him at the door to his office.

"I don't want to stay too long."

"Don't worry, the chief will call if he needs you to come back."

Inside the office hung several paintings Joe had handled for the lawyer. *Where can I get away from what happened?* He wanted to bolt. The sight of the lawyer in out-of-character Sunday-casual blue jeans and a Denver Broncos football jersey changed his mind.

"So what happened?"

Joe spelled out the few known details. The lawyer's pen scratched across the paper.

Joe took out his checkbook. "I'll return your payment, of course."

Dixon waved him aside. "Time for that later. They may recover the painting." He leaned back in his chair and looked toward one of Joe's favorite paintings, an abstract whose sharp lines and silver colors reminded him of the mountains. "You know I defend criminals. Over the years I have gained a little insight into how they think."

Is he saying he would represent the person who robbed the store? He can't. Conflict of interest.

"One thing that keeps me going—besides the concept that they are all innocent until proven guilty and they have the right to the best defense I can offer—is knowing the grace of God. When I represent them, I try to model His love and forgiveness. Every now and then someone listens and gets his life turned around."

Joe didn't want to think about the thief receiving grace. He should be punished.

"That's why I wanted the painting—a visual testimony to my clients that God is with them in what is for many their first brush with the law."

After that, Dixon spent time reviewing the insurance policy and going over the steps Joe would need to take. Some time later, someone knocked at the door, and Dixon let Michelle and Sonia in. He repeated his theory about Sonia's painting.

Sonia looked at Dixon with appreciation. "I agree. Maybe the thief needs the message of the painting more than any of us in this room."

Michelle squeezed Joe's hand, and he looked into the three concerned, hopeful faces, waiting for his reaction. Guilt, anger, fear—a multitude of emotions had washed over him at the invasion of his store. Most of all, he worried about how the robbery would affect the people closest to him, including these three people. Instead, they seemed to view the loss as an opportunity to trust God more.

Trust not in princes. . . . The Knight family motto came into his mind. All the information he had fed into his brain's computer clicked together and spit out the answer: his security didn't rest in time or place or people. It rested in God. Without God, he was crossing a high wire without a safety net.

Joy fizzed inside Joe and burst out in a bubble of laughter. He looked into Michelle's clear eyes, and his heart lightened, lighter than any time since the singing monk had taken Michelle's purse at the Renaissance Festival. If God—and the right woman—was for him, who could be against him? Amen.

❧

Michelle stayed through the long, difficult afternoon into the evening. How could she leave when Joe was so vulnerable, hurt, exposed? Once they had the okay, everyone returned to the store, and Sonia and Dixon made a list of missing items. The four of them shared supper at the steak place before going their separate ways.

"I'm glad you were here today." Joe held Michelle's arm as they walked up the driveway to the castle, gravel crunching underfoot.

She thought she heard all the things he didn't say. *I need you. You're important to me.* "I was glad I could help. Not that I did very much."

"You were there. That's what mattered."

"You're not as upset as I thought you would be." Something had broken loose during the meeting at Dixon's office. He appeared serene, for lack of a better word.

"God finally got it through my thick skull that my security comes from Him. It doesn't matter where I live or how careful I try to be. Bad things can happen. But God is always in control."

"God is always in control." Michelle repeated the words under her breath. She didn't fear for her physical safety—living on the edge for two years in Romania had cured any hint of that—but she did fear other things. Like failure. "I still need to learn that lesson myself. I'm glad you have peace about it." She lifted her hand to his face, as if to transfer his peace into her heart, and their faces drew together. They kissed, a joint affirmation and celebration.

By the time Michelle said good-bye to Nel and packed her things in her car, the hour approached nine o'clock. At this rate, Michelle would consider herself lucky if she got to bed before midnight. She shook her head and headed down the driveway. The car jerked over one of the stones lining the drive. A few yards later the rear end shimmied. *Oh no, not a flat.*

Michelle stopped the car and climbed out. Sure enough, the right rear tire wobbled in shreds along the ground. She opened the trunk and pulled out the spare and the car jack and hoped she could change the tire herself. She understood the concept well enough, but she hadn't changed a tire in years. Not since her father had first taught her how.

Light appeared at the castle door, and Michelle heard feet crunching on the gravel. She turned to see Nel approach. "I'll call Joe and tell him you have a flat."

Before Michelle could say no, Nel had gone back inside. A moment later, she reappeared at the door. "Come back inside while we wait."

Joe arrived about five minutes later and quick as a wink had the old tire off and had set the new tire in place. "When did you get this tire?"

"The garage that replaced my last flat had a spare on hand that they sold to me for ten bucks. I was grateful to get it." Michelle smiled as she remembered the Good Samaritan.

"I don't know how to tell you this." Joe sat back on his haunches. "But it's the wrong size tire. Almost right, but not quite. I'm afraid if I try to force it, I'll strip your lug nuts, and then you really would be in trouble."

What—

"Oh my." Nel pursed her lips in thought. "And the only garage that sells tires in town is closed for the night. In fact, I can't think of any place within fifty miles that would be open at this time of night."

Joe opened the door to the backseat and took out her overnight bag. "I'm sorry, but it looks like you're stuck here until the morning. Or I could drive you to Denver tonight, but you wouldn't have your car."

Morning—Michelle's mouth formed the syllables without uttering a sound. The thought of being late for work—again—

squeezed her heart with fear. "When do they open?" The answer to the question held her chances of success on the job.

"Between seven and seven thirty."

And Michelle had to leave by six to get to work on time. She called and left a message for Chavonne, telling her she'd experienced car trouble but expected to get there by ten. She fought the urge to overapologize, deciding explained tardiness would look better than no message at all. During the long, sleepless night Michelle went over every scrap of her last conversation with Joe. *Trust not in princes—or employers. My security is in God. But why would God lead me to this job only to let me fail through no fault of my own?*

But what if He did? The question refused to go away.

Just in case, Joe drove her to the gas station by half past six in the morning. The first attendant appeared at 7:15. He moved slowly, or so it seemed to Michelle, adrenaline pumping through her veins like a performance-enhancing drug. She paid a small fortune for a new tire and a spare, and Joe took her back to the castle. Half an hour later, she merged onto the highway. She parked in the multilevel garage near the office at close to ten.

A sad-faced Chavonne intercepted Michelle before she reached her desk. "Come with me."

They walked past cubicles filled with coworkers, past the copier and office supplies, past the secretary's desk, past Chavonne's own office to. . .Glenda Harris, senior vice president of personnel. The nervous ball in Michelle's throat formed tentacles, strangling her ability to speak.

"Sit down, Miss Morris." Ms. Harris spoke in brisk but not unkind tones. Chavonne took the seat next to Michelle and looked straight ahead, avoiding Michelle's eyes.

"Let's see. You've been with Mercury Communications for what, a month?" She studied the folder in front of her as if to refresh her memory. When she looked up again, all traces of kindness had disappeared.

"During that time, you have been tardy twice. And frankly, your work has been below standard. Mercury can't afford to carry extra weight. Your employment with this company is terminated, effective immediately."

twenty-one

Chavonne escorted Michelle to the exit, where the security guard took her ID badge.

"I'm sorry things didn't turn out better." Chavonne handed Michelle a box with the few personal items she had collected at her desk before disappearing behind a door that clanged like a prison. Only this jail locked her out, not in.

A security guard approached her. "Ma'am, you need to leave." She realized she was staring into empty space. She walked, almost ran, out the door and into the sunshine that mocked her pain.

She stashed her belongings in her car but didn't get in. She couldn't face Carrie with her failure yet. A right-hand turn brought her to the 16th Street Mall, and she meandered down the sidewalks. People in pin-striped suits hurried past, intent on business. Street performers—a saxophonist here, a guitarist there—plunked out tunes for a few coins in their hats. Giggling teenagers carried full shopping bags. She was the only one without a purpose, with nowhere to go.

She reached the end of the mall and wondered what to do next. In the distance she heard church bells ring, and she decided to find the place of worship.

Her steps led her up Colfax Avenue to a cathedral. A man with a weather-beaten face wearing too many clothes for the heat huddled on the front steps. A beggar's cup sat at his side, but he had focused his attention on a slice of bread he tore into pieces to toss to the pigeons gathered at his feet. "Beautiful day, ain't it?" His toothless grin held genuine warmth.

Michelle dug in her purse and tossed two quarters in his cup.

"God bless you, miss."

Michelle went inside. Perhaps a dozen people sat in the pews, causing her to wonder if she had interrupted a service in progress, but no one stood at the altar. They were probably people like herself, needing a quiet place to seek God's face.

The church must have seen every misery of the human condition, from the homeless man sunning himself on the front doorsteps to the oil barons who lost it all in the oil bust, from scared teenage mothers to senior saints who had outlived their children. Michelle's problem shrank back into perspective as she petitioned God not only for herself but for her fellow worshippers as well. She poured out her feelings.

I failed, Lord.

I love you, child.

I thought You led me to that job. Did I misunderstand, or did I screw it up all on my own?

I will never leave you nor forsake you.

God never answered the "why" questions, Michelle mused. He said, "I am God. Trust Me." She slipped out of the church, found a phone, and called Carrie.

"I was just leaving to take Viktor on a picnic. He's bursting at the seams with energy."

Michelle checked her watch, surprised to discover the lunch hour had arrived. Her spirits lowered a fraction. If she ever needed to talk with Carrie, to get a good dose of her cheerful good sense, today was the day.

"Tell you what." Carrie interrupted Michelle's thoughts. "We can go to Washington Park. You should be able to meet me there and get back to work in an hour."

"Sounds good." Michelle would explain about the job when they met.

Carrie gave Michelle directions to the park, and they met fifteen minutes later. Carrie had packed an extra lunch for Michelle, and the three of them quickly polished off the food. Carrie also dug out a water bottle and a sun visor for Michelle.

"I don't suppose you have another job in your magic bag, do you?" Michelle sounded wistful, even to herself. "They fired me today."

Carrie stared at her. "Oh no. I'm so sorry." They started down the trail that circled the large pond, talking about odds and ends.

Not many people ventured outside in the heat of a summer afternoon, and they met no one on the trail. Michelle wiped sweat from her face. Viktor rode ahead on his tricycle and then waited for them to catch up. They paused by a flock of geese.

"This reminds me of the day the agency turned down my application to adopt a child." Carrie tossed a few remnants of their lunch to the geese. "I went to a park like this one in Bucharest. I almost kidnapped a baby that day."

"What?" Michelle had never heard this part of the story.

"Yup. I was so desperate for a child that I wanted to make things happen my own way. But God didn't let me." She took a long swig from her water bottle. "It's one of those old but true sayings. God never closes one door without opening another. Whatever God has for you will be far better than what you had at Mercury. Like God giving me both Viktor and Steve. So much more than I asked for. And He will supply your needs."

God always opens a door. Something triggered in Michelle's brain, a suggestion she had rebuffed at the time. God had already opened the next door. She had a lot of phone calls to make when she got home.

❧

What a week. On Thursday morning, Joe gave his store a final check. Because of the minimal structural damage, he had only needed to clean and restock his shelves. *Only.* The extra pieces he had bought at the Cherry Creek Arts Festival would come in handy. He called his best-selling artists and begged them to send some more soon as possible.

He had also installed an alarm system. Trust in God and be prepared. He should have done it before.

Joe studied the effect of the new display, disappointed in spite of his best efforts. The current pieces of art didn't quite reflect the quiet quality people had come to expect from the Trojan Horse. He had lost so much more than money.

I'm being too critical of myself. God will provide. He always has. Joe replaced the CLOSED UNTIL FURTHER NOTICE sign on the front door with GRAND REOPENING.

A steady stream of customers kept him busy all day. *There's no such thing as bad publicity, they say.* People curious about the break-in, businessmen worried about the prosperity of downtown Ulysses, concerned friends and neighbors—all those and more came through.

The last customers left after six, and Joe evaluated the day. Among the many well-wishers, serious buying had taken place, twice a normal day's business. *Thank You, Lord.*

He grabbed a can of Dr Pepper from the refrigerator and stretched out his legs, relishing the successful day. He could take the store in a new direction now, maybe work with the town council to develop an artist-in-residence program. He sketched out a number of ideas and cost estimates.

The phone rang. *Maybe it's Michelle.* Her week-long silence had surprised and hurt him. *Probably wrapped up in her job again.*

Judy was calling. "Something has come up at the office.

Can you come by tomorrow morning about eight o'clock?"

"I'm going to see you at Mother's tomorrow night. Can't it wait until then?"

"No. It's rather urgent."

"Can I swing by tonight, then? I was planning on getting to the store early tomorrow."

"Sorry. We won't have the details until morning."

"I'll try to make it." He crossed fingers behind his back, not really intending to go.

"Promise me you'll be there." More than a hint of panic colored Judy's voice, intriguing Joe. What did his brother and sister-in-law have up their sleeves?

"All right, all right. I promise."

Because of the changed plans, he stayed late to get the store in order for tomorrow's business. At home he fell into a contented, if exhausted, sleep and woke late, putting on a T-shirt from Taos, New Mexico, with blue jeans. He made it to Brian's office a few minutes after eight.

The door swung open at his touch, but he saw no one. "Hi, it's me. What was so important?" He walked across to the room where he heard the whirring of a copier and pushed open the door.

Instead of Judy's red-gold mop, a sheet of hair as golden as corn silk swayed as the woman bent over the copier. *Michelle?* She pirouetted like a model on a runway, presenting herself for his inspection.

"Hi there, Joe. I'm the important business. Hope you're not disappointed."

"But. . .what? How?" Joe struggled to put his jumbled thoughts into words. "What are you doing here? In Brian's office? On a weekday? What about your job?"

"They fired me."

Joe opened his mouth to offer his sympathy, but

contentment oozed from Michelle, as if the termination brought her peace.

"I soon realized I had unfinished business in Ulysses. I'm here in Brian's office because I accepted his job offer. I'm his new office manager so that Judy can concentrate on being a full-time nurse."

"You decided to move to Ulysses? Permanently?" Joe couldn't believe what he heard, like winning a contest someone else had entered on his behalf.

"I sure did. Like you, I realized my security has to rest in God, not the place I worked, and after that, details don't matter." She grinned. "Aren't you going to ask me what my unfinished business is?"

A wild hope sprang up in Joe, almost choking his voice. "Do you mean—"

"I do. Why don't you stop staring and kiss me, my beloved husband-to-be? That is, if you still want me."

"I do." Joe took Michelle in his arms, sealing their promise with a kiss, a song telling plainly of God's love and peace ringing in his heart.

A Letter To Our Readers

Dear Reader:

In order that we might better contribute to your reading enjoyment, we would appreciate your taking a few minutes to respond to the following questions. We welcome your comments and read each form and letter we receive. When completed, please return to the following:

Fiction Editor
Heartsong Presents
PO Box 719
Uhrichsville, Ohio 44683

1. Did you enjoy reading *Plainsong* by Darlene Franklin?
   ❑ Very much! I would like to see more books by this author!
   ❑ Moderately. I would have enjoyed it more if

   _____

   _____

   _____

2. Are you a member of **Heartsong Presents**? ❑ Yes ❑ No
   If no, where did you purchase this book? _____

   _____

3. How would you rate, on a scale from 1 (poor) to 5 (superior),
   the cover design? _____

4. On a scale from 1 (poor) to 10 (superior), please rate the
   following elements.

   ____ Heroine   ____ Plot
   ____ Hero   ____ Inspirational theme
   ____ Setting   ____ Secondary characters

5. These characters were special because? _____

_____

_____

6. How has this book inspired your life? _____

_____

_____

7. What settings would you like to see covered in future
   Heartsong Presents books? _____

_____

_____

8. What are some inspirational themes you would like to see
   treated in future books? _____

_____

_____

9. Would you be interested in reading other **Heartsong
   Presents** titles? ❑ Yes ❑ No

10. Please check your age range:
    ❑ Under 18   ❑ 18-24
    ❑ 25-34   ❑ 35-45
    ❑ 46-55   ❑ Over 55

Name _____

Occupation _____

Address _____

City, State, Zip _____

E-mail _____

SIMPLE CHOICES

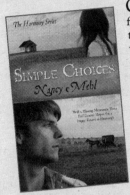

Can city-girl Gracie Temple find contentment in the small town of Harmony, Kansas—or will unexpected events have her running back to Wichita? When graphic designer Gracie brings rebellious Hannah Mueller, the pastor's daughter, home from art classes in the city, trouble follows. Hannah goes missing, and it's hard for Gracie to ignore the recent news stories about young girls disappearing elsewhere. Is Hannah another victim or just another runaway? As Gracie struggles with the mystery of Hannah's disappearance, her wedding plans to Sam Goodrich become more and more complicated. Will all the trouble disrupt Gracie's chances of a happy marriage?

Historical, paperback, 320 pages, 5.5" x 8.375"
